ENCHANTMENT LAKE

ENCHANTMENT
LAKE

A
NORTHWOODS
MYSTERY

MARGI PREUS

University of Minnesota Press

Minneapolis · London

"Sleep" from *New Collected Poems*, by Wendell Berry (Counterpoint, 2012). Copyright 2012 by Wendell Berry. Reprinted by permission of Counterpoint.

"The Peace of Wild Things" and "To Know the Dark" from *The Selected Poems of Wendell Berry*, by Wendell Berry (Counterpoint, 1999). Copyright 1999 by Wendell Berry. Reprinted by permission of Counterpoint.

Published by the University of Minnesota Press
111 Third Avenue South, Suite 290
Minneapolis, MN 55401–2520
http://www.upress.umn.edu

Design and production by Mighty Media, Inc.
Interior and text design by Chris Long

Library of Congress Cataloging-in-Publication Data

Preus, Margi.
Enchantment Lake : a Northwoods mystery / Margi Preus.
ISBN 978-0-8166-8302-4 (hc)
[1. Mystery and detective stories. 2. Lakes—Fiction. 3. Buried treasure—Fiction.
4. Great-aunts—Fiction. 5. Swindlers and swindling—Fiction. 6. Minnesota—Fiction.] I. Title.
PZ7.P92434Enc 2015
[Fic]—dc23
2014042651
Printed in the United States of America on acid-free paper
The University of Minnesota is an equal-opportunity educator and employer.

21 20 19 18 17 16 15   10 9 8 7 6 5 4 3 2 1

To my friends and family at Kabekona,
none of whom are in this story

There is a lake
I know the road along the shore
the turns you take
before it brings you to the door
I know the silence of the snow
the ice that cracks, the winds that blow
I know where fish hide in the weeds
I know where one small river leads
the red-winged blackbird on the reeds
There is a lake

—from the song "C'est toi mon lac,"
by Joel Preus

CONTENTS

I

DROWNING

Drowning, Francie thought. That's what this was like. You plunged into the cool, quiet darkness of the theater from the hot, bright street and sank into the gloom of the back rows of the house. And waited. Waited for the air to be squeezed, slowly but surely, from your lungs. Waited while your nerves frayed. Waited for your turn to audition.

From here, the voices on stage were like those on a distant shore, calmly conversing while Francie struggled, unobserved in the darkness, to keep her head above water. Her chest hurt, and something gnawed at the lining of her stomach. Everyone else got butterflies in their tummies when they were nervous, but no, she got hungry caterpillars instead, chewing holes in her stomach and . . . buzzing?

No, that was her phone. She pulled it out of her pocket, noticed the area code, and stepped into the lobby.

"Aunt . . . Astrid?" she whispered.

The voice on the other end cut in and out, so Francie stepped outside into the bright sun and jarring noise of the Manhattan

street. She plugged her traffic-facing ear and pressed the phone closer to her other one. "What?" she said. "It sounded like you said 'Someone is frying two grilled auks.'"

Car horns trilled, a siren wailed, and down the street a jackhammer beat out a mind-numbing rhythm. In between, Francie picked out words. Had her aunt said *danger?* And then, *murmur?* Or . . . *murder?*

There was a sudden freakish lull in the noise, during which the voice on the other end finished by shouting, "Come quickly!"

Come quickly? Francie was a thousand miles away! What was this about? Grilling auks? Her great-aunts were a little wacky, but they didn't make prank telephone calls. There was only one possibility: trouble. Her temples throbbed. Maybe *bad* trouble.

She dialed the number, but no one picked up. With every unanswered ring, her heart hammered harder, keeping time with the jackhammer down the street. Where had her great-aunt called from? she wondered. She didn't think either one of her aunts had a cell phone, and there was no phone at the cabin as far as she knew.

She glanced at the theater. It must be almost time for her audition. She could try calling back afterward, she supposed. But what if . . . ?

She punched in 911. "I think my great-aunts might be in trouble," she told the dispatcher, going on to explain that her elderly aunts lived on a remote lake in northern Minnesota. "I'm not sure what kind of trouble," Francie answered the dispatcher's question. "We had a bad connection." Could the NYPD contact the police in Walpurgis? she asked. No, Francie didn't know. She told the dispatcher she didn't know that, either. No, she didn't know! Why did they keep asking her questions instead of doing something about her aunts, whose lives might be in imminent danger?

Next she dialed the Walpurgis police department. The phone rang and rang. How could nobody be there? Not even any voice mail? What kind of police department didn't answer the phone?

Finally, she called her grandfather.

He laughed—laughed! "You know your aunts," he drawled, dragging the words out. "Don't you remember the summers you spent with them when you were younger? Loonie birds, the pair of them! I'm sure they're fine."

"Then why would Astrid say they were in danger?" Francie shouted into the phone. "And that there was a murder?" She wasn't positive that's what her aunt had said, but she was pretty sure.

"What did she actually say, Francesca?" her grandfather asked.

"She said . . ." Francie stopped and pressed her fingers to her forehead. She could hardly tell him they were grilling auks. Had Astrid said, "Someone is frying two grilled auks?" Or had she said, as Francie now told her grandfather, "Someone is . . . Trying. To. Kill. Us."

"She said that?" her grandfather asked.

"I *think* that's what she said."

"You *think* that's what she said."

"Well," Francie admitted, "we had a bad connection."

He laughed again. "I'm sure they're fine," he said.

Francie sighed. How could he be so relaxed about this? What if they really were in danger? She couldn't bear the thought of it. They were almost the only family she had left. Maybe she hadn't seen them in a while, a long while, but she'd always known they were there for her. Perhaps it was her turn to be there for them.

"I'm going to check up on them," Francie said.

"Now, don't get any funny ideas, Francesca. Francesca?"

But she wasn't listening. She had already shoved the phone

into her pocket and was moving steadily down the street. *Where am I going?* she wondered.

Home, she thought. I'm going home. Home to the apartment she shared with three other girls? Or home to the lake?

As she dodged pedestrians and wove through stalled traffic, she thought of frothy whitecaps on a wind-blown lake, the slam of a screen door, a sun-dappled path. She remembered swimming under bottle-green water and summer days that did not seem to end, the sun lingering in the sky as if it could not bear to leave.

Home, she thought. I'm going home to the lake.

2

WALPURGIS

THE TRIP WAS AGONY—everything was taking too long! She couldn't help imagining the worst scenarios. All the way through security: what if something horrible had happened? During the long flight: if her aunts' lives were in danger, what did she think she was going to be able to do about it, anyway?

And now the interminable bus ride, every mile of which was agony—the lurching stop it made in every little town, the blast of hot air as the door clattered open, the clamor of people getting on or off—made her grit her teeth in frustration. *Couldn't this bus go any faster?*

She pressed her nose to the cool glass of the bus window and watched as first the city, then the suburbs and their crop-like rows of houses gave way to rows of corn in rolling, open farm country. Gradually, the undulating fields studded with oaks and maples were swallowed by forests of spruce and pine. Here and there a lake glinted through the trees like a sequined cocktail dress glimpsed through a crowded room. She felt her pulse race. Soon there.

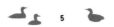

How long had it been? She hadn't been back since the Accident. That was seven years earlier, when she'd been ten. Now she was seventeen.

She gazed past the billboards and hand-painted signs (*God Loves You Country Inn; Oops, You Just Passed Gas!*) and at the birch trees flashing by, the white skin of their trunks bright in the afternoon sun. As a kid, she'd tried to imagine what this country must have looked like hundreds or even thousands of years ago. Or at least before there were billboards and cell towers.

She glanced at her phone. Her grandfather had called. She didn't intend to call him back. He would freak if he knew what she was up to. He didn't know she'd ditched out of summer school, left the city completely, and was almost to the lake. If she told him, he'd probably threaten to cut off her funds.

Her friends, on the other hand, would not be surprised that she had bought a plane ticket from New York to Minneapolis, and, too young to rent a car, hopped on a bus, and now . . .

How *was* she going to get to the cabin? She hadn't really thought through that part. She checked the map app on her phone and smiled. There was still no way to get where she was going, at least not by car—there was still no road on that side of the lake. She wondered if there was still no electricity, either. No phones. No Internet. No cell service. That's the way it had been seven years ago. She wondered how much might have changed since then.

Walpurgis, the sign read, *Population 2,020.*

The bus unloaded its handful of passengers at a gas station and pulled away. She shouldered her pack and started her hike down the main street, a string of gift shops displaying bears and ducks and moose in all manner of unlikely poses—as wine racks, coffee tables, lamps, pillows, and cookie jars. As she craned her neck to look at one extraordinarily jam-packed display, musing that there must be more moose in that one window than in the entire northwoods, she smacked headfirst into someone.

"Sorry," she mumbled at his chest, then glanced up.

Francie tried not to stare, first at his head of tousled, sun-bleached hair, then at the way he filled his shirt, and then at the big bouquet of flowers he carried, which for a moment she fantasized was for her. He gave her a little nod and smile, which, she had to admit, caused her stomach to flutter, and she couldn't help glancing—okay, staring—at him as he continued down the street.

The sun was hanging low in the sky by the time she reached Sandy's Beach Resort. Francie noticed the apostrophe and final "s" had fallen off his sign, so now it read *Sandy Beach Resort on Enchantment Lake*. As a service to the cabin owners on the other side of the lake, where there was no road, Sandy offered delivery service, dockage, and boat rides.

The half-log siding on the store had been replaced by half-log *vinyl* siding. Still, inside, the same big cast-iron sinks swarmed with minnows, leeches, and shiners. An old cooler, its light flickering, held bottles, not cans, of the soft drinks she had grown up calling "pop" but had learned to call "soda."

"Help you with something?" a voice asked. She turned, and there, stacking cans on a shelf was not Sandy but—what was his name?—Sandy's son, older now, of course.

"French Fry?" the young man said, blinking. His eyes were a curious mix of blues that shifted like the lake on a windy day.

"Wow," she said. "You not only remember me, you remember my nickname?"

"How could I forget little Frenchy?"

Francie noticed that his face, lit up from the soda machine, seemed to be glowing.

"Sandy?" Francie asked. She couldn't remember his name. "You know my great-aunts, right?"

"Of course!" he said, "Everybody knows Astrid and Jeannette."

"Are they okay?"

"Okay?" Sandy asked. The blue of his eyes shifted to a darker shade.

"They said someone was trying to kill them."

Sandy gave a low whistle. "That's crazy. But you do know that your aunts—"

"Are a little nutty?" Francie finished his thought.

"Well . . ."

"I know, but I couldn't help worrying."

He placed a few cans on the shelf and said, "I haven't seen them for a few days." Then, glancing at Francie, he added, "I'm sure they're okay, though. Don't worry." Sandy picked up the empty box at his feet and said, "Come on. I'll take you over there. Just give me a minute to close up. I'm the only one here."

Francie walked out on the dock and tapped her foot impatiently. In the evening sunlight, the lake was like . . . well, it was like a pool of molten gold, she supposed. The word "luminescent" came to mind, as if it were lit from beneath. Almost as if, Francie thought, there was a dragon's lair of gold under the lake, and the light was its reflected luster.

She wished she could be awed by it, but knowing that her aunts were across the lake, somehow relying on her to help them, she couldn't keep her thoughts on anything except getting there. She caught a whiff of the smells she remembered from her childhood: pine and lake and fresh air—and gasoline, probably from the gas can Sandy was hoisting into a big, fancy powerboat.

The boat reminded Francie of the ones the bad guys used in James Bond movies. She wondered what had happened to the old aluminum fishing boats with the ten-horse Johnson motors on the back.

"This is a fishing boat?" she asked Sandy as he lowered the boat from the lift.

He nodded.

"Are the fish faster nowadays?"

He laughed. "Naw, just gotta get to 'em before anybody else does." He winked. He had a cute dimple in one cheek, she noticed.

"What about that one?" She pointed to an enormous speed-boat on a lift nearby.

"Buck's," he said, his smile fading.

Sandy helped her into the boat, offering his hand in a sweetly old-fashioned way. "I hear you're a big detective in New York," he said.

She laughed and started to say no, whatever gave him that idea, but he'd started the motor, and Francie didn't want to shout over the noise, so she let it go. Sandy expertly spun the boat around, faced it toward the far shore, and, with motor roaring, sped out across the lake.

The boat went so fast it squeezed tears from Francie's eyes and whipped them behind her. Light from the setting sun flashed on the edge of the boat's wake, bright and hard as knife blades. Francie glanced back at the receding shore and was surprised to see so many imposing houses, with picture windows big enough to flatten flocks of geese. When did those get built? Along with the houses came the requisite jumble of boat launches, docks, pontoon boats, Jet Skis, and rafts. Also new: a huge, blinking cell phone tower. *Ugly* was her first thought. *Hey, maybe there's cell service here now* was her second. She checked her phone. Dead. She should have thought about that.

On the other hand, the approaching shore was just as she remembered it. From here it looked like a thick ruff of trees, with a few tiny cabin windows winking in the sun.

"Is this shore really enchanted like they say?" she asked as the boat slowed. "Why hasn't it changed the way the other side has?"

"It's probably because there's no road on this side of the lake—yet. But there's some kind of a fight over it. Some folks are pretty riled." Sandy made an expert landing at her aunts' dock.

"What do I owe you for the ride?"

"Ah, forget it, Frenchy," he said, blushing. "Do you want me to come with you to check on your aunts?"

"No." Francie stepped out onto the dock. "You need to get back to the store. I'm sure everything is fine. Sorry I called you Sandy," she added. Scott, that was his name.

"No, it's okay. That's what everybody calls me since I've taken over."

"Did your dad retire?"

"He died," Sandy said. "Deer hunting trip."

"Oh!" she said. "Was he . . . did he . . . ?"

"Did he get shot? No. Heart attack," Sandy shoved the boat away from the dock. "That's what they say, anyway."

That's what they say? Francie opened her mouth to ask him to explain, but Sandy had started the motor, and she knew he wouldn't hear her.

"There's been some strange stuff going on around here," he hollered over the roar of the motor. He wheeled the boat around and called back to her, "Be careful!" The boat sped away, quickly becoming a small, receding spot.

3

AT THE CABIN

FRANCIE STOOD FOR A MOMENT listening to the boat's wake wash against the shore. It had always struck her as a lonely sound and seemed even lonelier now that she was by herself. Maybe she should have asked Sandy to come with her. Why had she said no?

It was eerie how silent everything was. Once the lake was still again and the boat long gone, it was too quiet. No slamming of screen doors or squeals of kids playing in the lake, of parents calling their children home for dinner. But perhaps those were just sounds from her memory, when she and her brother had spent summers here, and they had been the ones making all the noise.

She walked slowly up the rather rickety stairs from the shore to the cabin, trying to reimagine the stillness as tranquil, peaceful. She concentrated on the air, soft on her skin, inhaled the scent of cedar and sun-warmed pine and the distinctive smell of the cabin that had always meant home to her. She took a deep

breath, taking in the musty, musky, wood-smoke, piney smell of it all. There *was* pleasure in being back—but also pain.

She had loved this place when she had been a kid, but a lot had happened since then. Things were different, and she had changed. She was a city girl now.

The way the door swung open—it hadn't been fully latched—made her throat tighten. Sandy's admonition to "be careful" came back to her. Why hadn't she asked about the "strange stuff" he said was going on?

The living room was suffused with light. The sun set directly across the lake, and at this time of the evening, the cabin was filled with a powerful orange glow that momentarily blinded her. When her eyes adjusted, she took in the scene: the same lumpy old couch, the creaky old rocking chair, the old fireplace, the old table covered with a half-finished jigsaw puzzle.

She was about to speak her aunts' names, although they seemed stuck in her constricted throat, when a small noise made her jump. Francie held her breath, her skin prickling. There it was again, coming from the kitchen. A mouse?

She fought back the urge to bolt and, holding her breath, crept toward the kitchen, then paused. Did she dare go a step farther?

One more step, around the corner, and she clutched at her chest. A body—well, part of a body—was sticking out of the re-frigerator, the rest swallowed up inside.

Gas! The fridge was gas, because there was no electricity here. She knew people used to commit suicide by sticking their heads in old-fashioned gas ovens. Was it possible to *kill* someone by sticking her head in an old-fashioned gas refrigerator? Francie's skin went as cold as if *she* had been refrigerated; she was unable to utter a sound.

Then one of the legs twitched. Had she imagined it? But no, a shelf in the fridge rattled, and there was a curse from a muffled voice, an "Oh, for the love of Mike!" And then, "Is that you, Astrid? Can you help me out here?"

Francie took a ragged breath. "Auntie Jen?" she squeaked. "Is that you?"

"Frenchy? Is that little Frenchy?" Jeannette said, without moving. Why didn't she come out?

"Are you okay?" Francie asked.

"No!" Jeannette cried. "My hair is stuck in the cheese drawer or something."

"Oh!" Francie exclaimed. She carefully stepped over the various containers of food scattered on the kitchen floor and reached in and untangled her aunt's curls from one of the metal racks.

"Oof!" Jeannette said, as she emerged, rubbing her head. "I was stuck good!"

Francie started giggling, and that made Jeannette giggle, and that made them both laugh harder, and pretty soon they were having a good cry.

Jeannette wiped her eyes and reached out to embrace Francie. "Dear little Frenchy! Look at you! So grown-up! Look at your beautiful black hair, with the white streak, just like—well, isn't it lovely? Gotten so tall! My, but you look grown-up."

Francie was used to that. Everyone assumed she was older than her age; she supposed because of the silvery streak in her otherwise black hair.

They babbled back and forth; Francie politely ignored the oblique reference to her mother, who had also had a white streak in her hair—about the only thing Francie knew about her. Finally, Francie said, "How long have you been stuck in the refrigerator? Is that why you sent for me?" she joked. "To untangle your hair?"

"What?" Jeannette said.

"Never mind. I'm so happy to see that you're okay! But tell me what's going on around here."

Jeannette glanced at the mess on the kitchen floor and said, "Oh, I have to go through the fridge once in a while and throw things out. You know your Aunt Astrid—she never throws away anything. Honestly, someday she's going to poison someone!"

"So Aunt Astrid is fine, too?" Francie began, then noticed a head of white hair floating by outside the kitchen window. And suddenly, Astrid was there, striding into the cabin.

There were more hugs and tears and cooing from both aunts and plenty of exclamations about how beautiful Frenchy had grown up to be, such an elegant creature, well, wasn't she lovely? And so on.

While basking in the compliments, Francie assessed her great-aunts. She had remembered Jeannette as a towering figure, somber and grandmotherly. She now seemed lovely and wise and kindly. And shorter than Francie now. She was still robust, though now her hair was more white than black; wisps of it floated about her like smoke.

Astrid had always been small, but now she seemed elfin, with bright white hair and even brighter blue eyes and a playfully wicked smile—something Francie had not noticed as a kid.

Although they'd obviously aged, Francie saw the same smiles, the same crinkle of the eyes, and heard their still youthful voices, especially when they laughed, although with a little waver (Jeannette) or a bit of a rasp (Astrid).

"Now," Francie said, "can you please tell me what's going on?"

"It looks to me like Jeannette is throwing out perfectly good food again," Astrid said, eyeing the contents of the refrigerator spread out on the floor.

"Actually, I was referring to your phone call—." Francie began.

"Oh yes, *that*," Jeannette said, picking up containers from the floor.

"Well?" Francie prodded.

"We'll tell you all about it, but first let's get some food in you, poor thing. Coming all that way—you must be starving!"

Francie started to object but then realized she'd had only a couple tiny bags of airplane peanuts and a Coke all day, and she *was* starving. "Okay, yes, I am hungry," Francie admitted, "but can you explain things while we're fixing dinner?"

"No," Jeannette said. "You sit there and tell us all about yourself."

"But I want to know what's going on with you."

"You first," Jeannette insisted.

Over the next hour, between bites of fiery hot curry and pickled beets—and reminiscing about some of the more unusual meals they'd had when she was a kid—they asked about her life in New York, and she heard about their life at the lake and winters in New Mexico. They asked after her brother, about whom she knew painfully little, she was sorry to admit.

Finally, Francie's patience came to an end. "Please, Aunties, will you *please* tell me what is going on! What was that phone call about?"

"Frenchy," Astrid said, her eyes dancing, "there's a mystery here. And we think you're the only one who can solve it." She got up and bustled over to the cupboards.

"Me? What makes you think I can solve anything?" Francie said. "And what are you doing?"

"You were always very keen on solving mysteries when you were little." Astrid's voice was muffled, her head deep in a cupboard.

Francie snorted. "I was a kid! And what are you looking for, anyway?"

"I'm looking for some bars," Astrid said.

"Oh, boy," Jeanette murmured. "I better go give her a hand." She hoisted herself out of her chair, then turned to Francie and added, "You worked very hard to find the buried treasure, remember?"

"Yes," Francie said, "and I didn't find it, either. Remember that part?"

"I'm sure you came very close, though," Astrid said, opening and shutting drawers and cupboards in somewhat useless fashion. "The legend of the treasure that lies 'under enchantment,'" she said, waving a wooden spoon as if it were a magic wand. "Did you ever figure out whether it was under enchantment, as in 'bewitched'? Or was it under *Enchantment,* as in under the lake?"

"I never solved that or anything else," Francie said. "And I'm unlikely to be able to solve your mystery, either." She gritted her teeth, trying not to regret the audition she'd missed, and removed herself from the kitchen.

"So you don't even want to know what the mystery is?" Astrid called after her.

Alone in the living room, Francie indulged herself in some eye rolling. "Okay, fine," she said. "What's the mystery?"

"It's about the road!" Astrid chirped.

"We don't know that," Jeannette snapped. She came out to the living room and set down a plate of bars on the coffee table while Astrid carried a pot of tea and three cups.

"What road?" Francie asked. She eyed the bars, wondering what they were made of. Perhaps that was the mystery, she thought.

"They're talking about putting in a road on this side of the lake," Astrid said. "We don't know who's behind it, but we suspect that the road might have something to do with the fact that someone is trying to kill us."

"Kill you!" Francie exclaimed. So she *had* been right. Take *that,* Granddad!

"When she says 'us,'" Jeannette said, "she means 'us' in the larger sense."

Okay, hold on, Francie thought. Maybe Granddad was right.

Jeannette continued. "It seems that people along the lake-shore are . . . well . . ."

"They're dropping like flies!" Astrid crowed. She poured Francie a cup of tea.

"Not to be rude or anything," Francie said, "but my recollection is that a lot of the cabin owners here are kind of . . ."

"Old?" Jeannette asked.

Francie hesitated. "Yeah."

"They're not dying of old age, if that's what you're thinking," Astrid said.

"Then how?"

"Strange accidents," Astrid said. "Or *are* they accidents? That's the mystery for you to solve, and you are the perfect person, being a detective and all."

"Detective? You know that was a TV show, right? I played a detective on a TV show—a *kids'* TV show. That does not qualify me as a detective."

"Yes, yes, we know all that, but we always thought you *should* be a detective," Astrid said.

"And as long as you're here, there's someone we'd like you to meet," Jeannette added.

Francie felt frustration boiling up in her. "Aunties!" she croaked. "Do you realize how much of a scare you gave me? I thought your lives were in imminent danger! I was afraid you might be dead by the time I got here! I dropped everything, worried myself into a frenzy, and came all the way out here so . . . so you could set me up with a blind date?" Was she angrier with her aunts for duping her, she wondered, or with her grandfather for being right?

"Oh my," Jeannette said. "I just mean you shouldn't worry about *us*. Astrid and I aren't in any *immediate* danger, are we, Astrid?"

Astrid's eyes glittered. "Oh, but yes! Yes, I think so. I should think we are exactly the prime victims."

Wait. So they *were* in danger, after all? Francie watched Jeannette's eyes flash at Astrid. Was she scolding her for saying that? Or was it something else? There was a little crackle in the air; Francie almost felt the prickling of electricity but didn't know why. She supposed if she really *were* a detective, she would know what that feeling meant. But no, she was just confused. "So are you two in danger? Or not?"

"That's enough for one night," Jeannette said. "We old people need to toddle off to bed. We've prepared the boathouse for you."

"Wait a minute! First you aren't in danger, then you are, then, 'Let's all go to bed'?"

Astrid opened her mouth, but Jeannette stopped her, saying, "It will wait until morning. Here's a flashlight. And don't you worry. You're perfectly safe."

"I'm not worried for me," Francie said. "But what about you? I'm worried about you!"

"Oh, we're not in any danger tonight, we're quite sure," Astrid said.

"How can you be so sure?"

"Well, because you're here!"

Francie was not at all sure she provided any protection, especially if she was going to sleep in the boathouse, but both aunts shooed her toward the door, saying, "That's enough for tonight—good night!"

Just as she was going to step out, Francie noticed a gun leaning by the door. "A rifle?" Francie asked. "What's that for?"

"Jet Skiers," Astrid said and winked.

Francie must have looked alarmed because Astrid quickly added, "Oh honey, it's just a .22. It's for woodchucks. They're murder on our garden."

4

THE BOATHOUSE

THE BOATHOUSE had been Francie's favorite place to sleep when she was a kid, and her aunts remembered that. They must have known she would come back, too, because they'd obviously prepared it: the canoe had been taken out, the floor swept, the bed made up.

Lying in the creaky bunk with the windows open, only inches from the water, Francie tried to recall her childhood wonderment. But instead of feeling the magic of wind and waves, what she noticed was the insistent drone of mosquitoes on the other side of the screens, the scratching of a mouse somewhere, and the fading sound of a boat motor. Every so often there was a fizz, then a pop or a series of crackles—faraway fireworks before the Fourth of July.

Beyond all that was a deep and empty silence. No horns honking, sirens wailing, whine of tires, or clank of garbage trucks. No crashing of bottles in the alley dumpster at 2 a.m. Everything was utterly silent, so silent she could almost hear her heart beating. But no. Of course she couldn't.

Someone had once told her the story of the troll who had no heart in his body. "Far, far away there is a lake," the story went. "On that lake there lies an island, on that island stands a church, in that church there is a well, inside that well there swims a duck, and inside that duck there is an egg. Inside that egg lies the troll's heart."

Francie's heart was not tucked away in quite so complicated a way. She had long pictured it inside a small silver box, engraved all over in elegant, swirling designs. It was a specific box, one she'd played with when she'd been a kid: her mother's jewelry box. At least she had *pretended* it had belonged to her mother. Francie knew enough about anatomy—and reality—to know that it was far too small to contain a heart, and anyway, it was impossible. But that's how she pictured it: her heart encased inside this beautiful box, untouchable. Sometimes she imagined just the box inside her chest, where her heart should be. Sometimes, when she felt particularly lonely, she felt as if the box with her heart inside was somewhere else entirely.

A loon called. Then another, closer. Creak of bed as she shifted. Drone of mosquitoes. Bang of moth on screen.

"Far, far away there is a lake," she thought the story could go. "On that lake there is a loon, and inside that loon there is an egg, and inside that egg there is a box, and in that box there lies my heart."

A breeze kicked up. She heard it first in the highest boughs of the pines, then in the ticking of the poplar leaves, and finally in insistent little waves pushing up against the shore. And then:

Bing bing bong. Bong bong bing. Bing bing bong. And so on.

A wind chime.

Augh! What was the *point* of wind chimes? And this one was worse than most: pathetically tuneless, music with brain damage. *Bing bing bong. Bong bong bing.* After fifteen minutes of torture, she decided the noise must cease.

She rose, slipped on her flip-flops, and stepped out into the dark.

Except it really wasn't all that dark. The moon was up and almost full, or just past full, Francie wouldn't know. The moon was not something she often noticed in Brooklyn. But here, tonight, it was not to be ignored. She stood for a moment gazing at the lake, where moonlight rolled out in a long, glittering carpet.

She had a sudden memory of being in a boat with her father, dragging her hand in the water trying to catch the moonlight. But it eluded her, always just out of reach. The boat plunged on, the path of light continuing to retreat in front of her.

Bing bong bing.

Where *was* the blasted thing?

Bong bing bing.

Next cabin over. She started through the woods to the neighbor's.

Here the moon had been cut into abstract shapes and laid on the ground in fanciful designs. Francie had an impulse to play hopscotch on the bright patches, but reminded herself that she was *sneaking* to the neighbors. She tried to move quietly, but her flip-flops slapped her heels, sharply punctuating each step.

It didn't seem like the cabin was occupied, although through the trees she glimpsed what looked like a boat tied to the dock. But it was hard to know if people were here or not since there was no driveway and no car.

The tubes of the chimes gleamed in the moonlight, and she was happy to see she could easily slide them onto a convenient little shelf under the roof. The Olsons (did they still own this place?) might even think the wind had pushed the chimes up there.

Now the only sounds were the soft lapping of waves against the shore and the wind high up in the pine boughs, making a soft whoosh, and—what was *that*? Another sound, somewhere distant, though she couldn't tell from where, caught her ear: a harsh, metallic, rhythmic *ka-chink*. Chains? A boat winch? A car radio with just the bass audible? Whatever it was, she could only hear it when the wind lulled.

She strained to listen, but a movement, caught out of the corner of her eye, distracted her. Something seemed to have stepped into a shadow . . . deliberately? It was big enough to be a bear—or a man. A sudden chill cut through her thin summer nightgown.

Which would be better, she wondered, bear or man? She remembered that the bears around here were black and "small" and weren't supposed to be dangerous, compared to, say, a grizzly. That knowledge didn't seem to have a calming effect on the goose bumps that had risen all over her arms.

All the way back to the boathouse she told herself it was nothing. The strange sound could have been frogs. Frogs made all kinds of bizarre racket: chirping, croaking, quacking, peeping, and for all she knew, ka-chinking.

And the crunching of pine needles behind her? Her imagination for sure.

Even so, she couldn't shake the feeling that someone was watching her, and the back of her neck prickled. Some detective I make, she thought, scared of the dark.

Back in the boathouse, she settled into her creaky bunk and waited for her breathing to resume its normal pattern. Now the wind chime was silent, but the fireworks continued. There were distant pops, bangs, and occasional fizzes as the fireworks wound down.

A couple of big speedboats went by—one of them was Sandy's. She smiled because she hadn't lost her talent identifying boats by their sound. It was a skill she'd developed as a kid. Her dad used to tease her that she couldn't tell the difference between the call of a chickadee and the chirr of a red squirrel, but she could identify any motor on their side of the lake.

There was one loud pop, like a truck backfiring. I hope that's the last of the fireworks, she thought. Then, blessed silence.

5

SUICIDE WEATHER

"THEY'LL CALL IT SUICIDE, but it isn't," Astrid said the next morning, taking a sip of coffee.

Francie choked on her bite of toast. "What isn't suicide?"

"The shooting down the way. What do you think that loud bang was in the middle of the night?"

"Fireworks," Francie said.

Astrid set her cup in its saucer and pursed her lips in the same disappointed way she had when as a kid Francie sat on the nice furniture in her wet swimsuit. "All those *other* bangs were fireworks, but that one bang, in the very early morning hours, was a shotgun," Astrid said. "Cream?" she asked, pouring an impressive dollop of heavy cream in her own coffee.

"How do you know that?" Francie asked. She shook her head to the offered cream pitcher.

"I heard it. I guess I know a single shot from a .20 gauge when I hear one."

Francie wondered how her aunt was so well versed in the reports of firearms. She also wondered if her aunt was correct. If she was . . . Francie felt the now-familiar prickle at the back of her neck. Her feeling of unease was not soothed by the sight of a dark bank of clouds massing up on the western horizon.

"By the way," Francie said. "Where's Aunt Jen?"

"She's gone to find out what she can about the situation. As for you," Astrid said, "here's your assignment for today: go into town to Paradise Realty and set up an appointment."

"What kind of appointment?" Francie asked.

"An appointment with a real estate agent, a specific one. His name is Buck. Buck Thorne."

"Buck Thorne? That's a real name?" Francie said. "Like that invasive plant, *buckthorn*?"

Astrid nodded. "Tell him that your aunts—that's us—are going to leave the cabin to you, and you want to sell it as soon as we have passed away."

"Auntie! What is this about?"

The screen door banged and Jeannette walked in.

"Oh, dear," she said, wiping tears away, "it was Warren."

"Warren!" Astrid exclaimed. "Oh, how terrible!"

The sisters hugged each other, and Francie could see that a box of tissues would be needed. She retrieved one.

"Who would ever think he would commit suicide?" Jeannette said, reaching for a tissue.

"You know very well he didn't!" Astrid snapped.

Jeannette's mouth tightened.

"Should we call the police?" Francie asked.

Jeannette and Astrid exchanged looks.

"What?" Francie asked.

"Very funny!" Astrid said, blowing her nose.

"Can't you just hear Sheriff Rydell now?" Jeannette pulled more tissues from the box.

"*What?*" Francie asked more insistently. She couldn't tell if her aunts were crying or laughing at this point. It sounded like snuffling with an occasional guffaw thrown in.

"Rydell won't do anything," Jeannette said. "He never does. Everything is always an 'accident.'"

"Are you sure Warren *didn't* commit suicide?" Francie asked.

"Of course he didn't. He was perfectly happy," Astrid said.

"How do you know that?" Francie said. "Sometimes people suffer from depression and nobody even—"

"Not Warren. You didn't know him so you wouldn't know, but he was perfectly happy. Plus he was going to come over here on Wednesday and fix our drain. He wouldn't have killed himself before he took care of that," Astrid said.

"If you're that desperate, I think you cease caring about those sorts of things."

"Not Warren," Jeannette said. "He would have found a time that wouldn't have inconvenienced anyone. So, let's say he was murdered." She turned to Astrid. "Miss Smarty-Pants, *if* he was murdered, who did it?"

Astrid pursed her lips. "Yes . . . it doesn't quite make sense. If someone is trying to get rid of cabin owners, then why get rid of Warren? He doesn't even own a cabin!" Then she brightened. "Isn't it lucky that we have Frenchy here?" she turned to Francie. "What do *you* think?"

"I think I'll go make some inquiries." Francie really just wanted to go for a run and clear her head.

"Don't worry!" both aunts chirped. "You're perfectly safe!"

"I'm not worried," Francie said, and went out.

What was there to be worried about? Her aunts had some crazy paranoia going, right? So even people who committed suicide were part of some big murder plot. There was nothing to worry about! But as she jogged along the path, the ominous feeling she'd had the previous night seemed to roll over her the way the dark clouds were rolling across the lake.

As she ran on the path along the lakeshore, she tried to concentrate on the scent of pine needles underfoot and the charming sight of the cozy little cabins nestled in among the pines, all of them familiar to her from her childhood. In fact, most of them had been built decades ago and had remained in the same families through generations. There were a few first-generation owners still holding down their forts, watching their great-grandchildren who, lacking computers and TVs, played with the same dog-eared decks of cards and read the same comic books their parents had when they'd been young.

She would do a little snooping, she thought. Why not? Who along here might have been out in the middle of the night, she wondered. Who might have followed her? That is, *if* she had been followed. And as long as she was sleuthing, maybe she could learn a little about Warren. She might even try to find out something about these strange accidents her aunts talked about. And what was up with this road?

At the Angells', a young woman with impossibly long, lean, and tan legs was in the yard, standing over a patch of petunias with a watering can. Could it be the same gangly kid Francie had known as a girl, the one with braces and freckles who had always reminded her of a giraffe?

"Ginger?" Francie asked.

"Frenchy?" The girl turned and smiled; the braces were gone, replaced by perfect white teeth. "Hi! Wow! You're here! That's crazy! I hear you're a big detective in New York!"

Francie began to explain that she was not a detec—

"Something in my hair!" Ginger shrieked.

"Stand still," Francie told her, having spied the buzzing wasp caught in Ginger's thick curls. She carefully pulled strands of Ginger's hair apart, allowing the wasp to escape, both Ginger and insect unscathed.

"Wow," the relieved Ginger said. "Is wasp extraction a service of the NYPD? You did that like a pro."

"No," Francie laughed. She was about to explain once again that she had no connection with the NYPD, when a filthy little boy, about eight years old, appeared.

"Remember my brother?" Ginger asked. "Pigpen?"

The little brother frowned. "That's not my name. My name is Timothy James."

"Nice to meet you, Timothy James," Francie said.

"Just call him T.J.," Ginger said.

Next, a big, shaggy black mutt trotted up. "This is Rusty," she added. "Guess which one likes to dig in the dirt."

"Not the dog?" Francie guessed.

"Correct," Ginger said, and then to her brother, "Find any elephant bones lately?"

T.J. scowled at her and shimmied up a tree.

"I didn't think I'd be here this summer; I thought I'd get a job, but my mom had to work. T.J. begged and begged to spend the summer at the cabin, and mom said yes, as long as I'd stay with him."

"So you're up with your dad?"

Ginger shook her head and looked down.

"You're here by yourself? Your parents aren't here?" As she said it, Francie realized how funny it sounded. After all, she lived without parents, too. But in the city, not way out here in the woods.

"My mom has to work this summer," Ginger said, "on account of my dad."

"Your dad . . . ?" Francie asked.

"He died this spring," Ginger said.

"Gosh!" Francie said. "I'm so sorry! I didn't know."

"It was a shock to everyone. He came up earlier this spring to open the cabin and get the pump working and hook up the gas and all that, and the well had gone bad."

"Gone bad? What does that mean?"

"Poisoned!" she said.

"Someone poisoned the well?"

"No. I guess it just happens sometimes. A well goes bad, gets poisoned somehow. You can die from it. That's what happened to my dad. Since then everybody has had their water tested, but all the other wells are fine."

"That's strange."

"Yeah," Ginger agreed and sighed. "So my mom's selling. That's what I'm supposed to be doing here. Mom is paying me to babysit but also to paint and fix up. I'm spending the summer all by myself, a regular Pippi Longstocking. Just me and my monkey, Mr. Nilsson," Ginger added, pointing to T.J., who stuck his tongue out at her. "And Warren to help with the cabin stuff, thank goodness. He's coming over to fix a bunch of stuff this afternoon."

"Oh, Ginger," Francie said. "I'm sorry to be the one to tell you this, but Warren is, um . . ." Francie had never had to be the bearer of this kind of bad news before. How were you supposed to break this sort of thing gently?

Ginger stopped and looked at her, her dark eyes glowing somehow darker.

"Warren is . . . dead," Francie said finally.

"What?" Ginger said. "How? How do you know that?"

"My aunt Jeannette went snooping this morning." She explained the little she knew about the situation.

"But suicide?" Ginger shook her head. "That seems almost unbelievable. He said he'd be over today to fix my pump! It's so unlike him to say he'll do something and then not do it."

"That's just what my aunts said. And they don't think it was suicide, either," Francie added.

Ginger looked up at her. "What's the alternative?"

"The alternative is that somebody killed him."

"That's horrible! Who would do that? Everybody loved Warren. Well, everybody needed Warren. I don't know if everybody loved him."

"What do you mean?"

"I just mean that he was so aloof. Norwegian bachelor handyman. Who knew what he thought or felt about anything."

"Can I ask you something else?" Francie said. She cleared her throat. "Are you sure that your well just went bad—that it didn't have a little help?"

"Oh, you too?" Ginger cried. "Just like everybody around here, including the sheriff. You think my mom killed Dad."

"What? No!"

Ginger wasn't listening. She charged on: "The sheriff came out and made all kinds of insinuating remarks—as if she murdered Dad! Now everybody thinks she killed him, and that's part of the reason why she won't come up here."

"That's not what I—" Francie started again.

"Yes, they fought, but she wouldn't—didn't—kill him! That's just ludicrous."

"I didn't mean your mom," Francie explained. "What about someone else?"

"Someone else?" Ginger looked up, and for a moment their eyes met, in concern, worry, and maybe fear. Ginger shivered. "You're kinda creeping me out right now."

"Sorry," Francie said. "I'm sure it's nothing to worry about."

A sudden gust of wind blew some clothes off the line, and Ginger went to retrieve them. Francie waved good-bye and continued down the path.

Could Ginger's dad have been murdered? Francie wondered. And Warren? Was there a murderer on the loose, like her aunts seemed to think?

But if she had hoped to find a murderous type along the shore, she was disappointed. White-haired folks all along the lakeshore hailed her as she jogged by, and she was inevitably invited in. Pleasantries were exchanged, bars and cookies were consumed, Francie was assumed to be a detective, and everyone was devastated about poor Warren, until eventually conversation got around to the road and who was for or against it.

As far as she could tell, everyone was against it. Whose idea was it, anyway? Nobody seemed to know. Her curiosity about this, and about possibly finding a murder suspect, propelled her down the path, even after consuming five cups of coffee and one each of lemon bars, chocolate-chip cookies, fudge, powdered sugar donuts, and seven-layer bars. And a wedge of rhubarb dessert.

Evelyn Smattering crowed, "You're awfully young to be a detective!"

"No, Mrs. Smattering, I'm not a detective," Francie said, relieved that finally there was no interruption and she could explain. "I only played one on a TV show."

Mrs. Smattering stood back to regard her critically. "No. I watched that show and that wasn't you. You don't look anything like that girl."

"Of course, my hair was a different color and style, and people do look different on TV. Also, I was younger then."

Mrs. Smattering laughed. "Nope! You're nothing like her at all. Now, honey, would you like a slice of graham cracker pie?"

Francie ate a small wedge of pie—Mrs. Smattering was just as adamant about the eating of pie as she was about Francie's mistake in thinking she had ever been an actor on TV. She was so certain of it, in fact, that even Francie began doubting she had ever been on the show. It *had* been a bit of a dream, a short-lived but lovely dream. She had been on only a few episodes before the show was canceled. Still, for that little while, it had been wonderful to be able to tell people she was an actor and have it be true.

"Are you living all alone, Mrs. Smattering?" Francie asked. "Or does your son help out?"

"Kevin?" Suddenly her eyes looked enormous and frightened behind her thick glasses. "Kevin used to help out a lot. He was retired, you know. But this spring a tree limb fell during a storm—right there, where the little extra bedroom used to be. Crashed right through the roof. Killed him while he slept." She sighed. "Warren's been helping me now. Oh, dear . . ." she trailed off. "I'm not sure how much longer I can stay here. Don't tell anybody this, sweetheart, because I'm not supposed to tell *anybody*, but you being a detective and all, I'm sure you can keep secrets—"

"I'm not a detec—" Francie interrupted to say, but Mrs. Smattering just kept going.

"—I've already sold it," she finished.

"Sold it! When do you have to move out?"

"That's the best part!" Mrs. Smattering said triumphantly. "I don't! The fellow I sold it to said I could live here as long as I like."

"Who bought it? A friend or relative?"

"Oh, no!" Mrs. Smattering said. "I can't possibly tell you. I promised I wouldn't tell anyone!"

At the next cabin, a man, much younger than the usual crowd, stood sizing up a large dead tree in his yard.

"I used to be a tree hugger," he said after she greeted him. "Now it's me against the trees. Gotta figure out a way to get this one down without having it land on my shack."

"Are you a Potter?" she asked, remembering that this was the Potters' cabin.

"Yes," he said. "That is, I am a Potter and I am a potter. And everyone calls me 'Potter.' Ha!" He gestured to the side of the house where pots of all shapes and sizes were stacked—well, piled—in a jumbled heap.

"Those are rejects," he said, by way of explanation.

She could just make out a kiln in the backyard.

"Wow. You make your pots over here and have to take them by boat over there?" She pointed across the expanse of lake. "That must be tricky."

"I wait for a calm day."

He went back to cutting his tree, and Francie continued, glad that at least he hadn't invited her in for coffee.

"Delicate!" snorted Mrs. Hansen over tea and sandbakkels, when Francie mentioned the pottery. "Did you see any of them?"

"I just saw his reject pile."

Mrs. Hansen shook her head. "How Potter can make a living selling those clunky things, I'll never know."

Francie smiled and looked down into her dainty china cup. Compared to this china, his pottery would naturally look really primitive she supposed. It was probably a matter of taste.

Mrs. Hansen's husband, Wally, had drowned in a fishing accident just two months earlier—in May. Right around the same time as Ginger's dad, Francie noted.

The two of them stared out the window at the rain that had started to fall.

"I imagine," Mrs. Hansen said, "that he must have stood up to reel in a really big fish and been pulled over the side of the boat. Although he usually fished with a partner, that night he was alone. Well, I think he was alone. That's what everyone said."

Mrs. Hansen sighed. "At least he died doing what he loved. That's what people say, anyway. I guess it's supposed to be a comfort."

"It must be hard for you to be here without him," Francie said.

Mrs. Hansen nodded and said, "I've sold the place."

Big, fat drops of rain splatted against the picture window.

"Really?" Francie said. "I thought you loved it here."

"Yes, I do, but it's very hard to keep the place up without Wally. And now Warren's gone, too. Poor Warren."

"When will you move?" Francie asked.

"Oh!" Mrs. Hansen said, smiling. "I have a very special arrangement. I can stay here as long as I like. I can stay here until I die!"

PLANTATION PEOPLE

THE BRIEF RAIN had ended and the sun had come out, so Francie continued on, running again, hoping she'd be just a blur and unrecognizable. She jogged along the old familiar path, noticing that the trees seemed even bigger than she remembered. Well, trees never stopped growing, did they?

Of the people she'd met so far, only the potter and Ginger seemed young and spry enough to have followed her the previous night. The potter hadn't seemed the slightest bit interested in her, and Ginger was an old friend. As for murderers—she hadn't seen anyone who would fit that description.

Suddenly, the canopy opened, and Francie felt as if she had awakened sharply from a dream. Beyond the trees a lawn of lush, green grass all a-glitter from the recent rain seemed to roll on and on. A golf course? What *was* this place, she wondered as she stepped gingerly out of the trees onto the thick green carpet. The lawn ran down to the lake like an enormous carpet, unimpeded by trees, from an equally enormous southern-style mansion—a plantation house, but with decks instead of pillared porches.

How on earth did it get here? she wondered.

"The path goes around the back!" called a cheery woman's voice from one of the many decks. Francie looked up, half expecting to see Scarlett O'Hara in a hoop skirt and bonnet, but the voice came from someone who looked more like a Ralph Lauren model (a *mature* one) dressed casually, but elegantly, for the country, with the perfect hair, the perfect country look, and, Francie realized with a start, the perfect face. This woman was stunningly beautiful, and this was the weirdest part: familiar. Maybe she *was* a model!

"Hello, darlin'." The woman smiled down at Francie with an intelligent face—not a vacuous model, that's for sure. Who *was* she? "Out for a jog? That's so healthy!" the woman said.

"I don't remember this place from my childhood," Francie said. "Isn't this where the Simonsens' cabin used to be?"

"That's right," the woman said. "We built right after Mr. Simonsen passed away."

"Mr. Simonsen died? What happened? He wasn't that old, was he?"

"Not terribly old. He died of snakebite."

"Snakebite? But there aren't any poisonous snakes here, are there?"

"So they say. Isn't that the oddest thing?" She shouted suddenly, "MORTY, HONEY!"

A man's voice responded from a nearby outbuilding.

"What kind of snake was it that bit Simonsen?" the woman shouted again.

Another muffled reply.

"Oh, that's right," she said. "Water moccasin."

"Water moccasin! That's not possible. There aren't water moccasins this far north. How could that have happened?"

"Global warming? Ha ha! Just a little joke," the woman said, laughing a champagne-bubbly laugh. "Mmm. Not very funny, I guess. By the way, I'm Savery Frederickson, like 'savory' but with an 'e.' And you are . . . ?"

"Francesca Frye."

"Oh! You're the big detective from New York! So *young* to be a detective," Mrs. Frederickson clucked.

Francie was about to explain and then suddenly—she wasn't sure why—decided to let it go.

"So, my dear," Mrs. Frederickson leaned forward, her eyes glittering, "what are you investigating?"

"Ah." Francie was surprised to hear herself saying, "I, um, am looking into strange accidental deaths along the lakeshore." She seemed to feel a need to impress Mrs. Frederickson.

"How interesting!" Mrs. Frederickson exclaimed. "Have there been strange deaths along here—other than the snakebite, of course? We haven't heard."

"Yes, some," Francie said.

"Well!" Mrs. Frederickson said, "Do let me know how you get on, won't you? Funny. It seemed like such a quiet little corner of the world when we bought this place. Say, darlin', as long as you're here," she went on, "there is a question I'd like to ask you. There's only that one chunk of property between us and the road, you know." Mrs. Frederickson nodded her head toward the woods next door. And a river and a swamp, Francie thought, but didn't say. "That piece of property that belongs to your aunts. We've offered to buy it from them—I mean, do you really think they have any plans for it, at their age? We could continue the road through here—there are plenty of people who would like a road farther on, too, you know. Listen, can you talk some sense to your aunts? I can't see what they are doing with it except being stubborn. No hard feelings, I hope." Mrs. Frederickson went on without a break, "Listen, we're having a little gathering here tomorrow night. Our daughter Latice is also having some friends up from the Twin Cities, but it would be so nice if she could meet some young people along the lake. She'd be so delighted if you'd come to the party. Let me introduce you to her . . ."

Mrs. Frederickson continued talking as she walked Francie around the side of the house. A teenaged girl was sprawled on a reclining lawn chair in a bikini, pink as a pig on a spit, Francie thought. Mrs. Frederickson introduced Francie to Latice, then said, "Tomorrow night, remember! Let me know if you want a ride. We'll be picking everyone up on our pontoon, and we can pick you up, too, if you like."

Francie nodded, and Mrs. Frederickson wafted away, leaving her alone with Latice.

"Do you bleach your hair to get it to do that?" was the first thing out of Latice's mouth. She didn't bother to sit up, but squinted at Francie from her reclining position.

"No, it does this on its own," Francie explained. She was used to people staring at the white streak in her hair, but most people didn't ask outright if she dyed it. She knew it made her look older than her age. Sometimes she thought it even made her *act* older than her age.

"Huh," Latice said. She didn't believe Francie, and Francie didn't care.

"How do you like the lake?" Francie asked.

Latice growled, "Everybody goes to their lake places for a week or something, but nooo, we have to practically *live* here."

"You don't like it, I take it," Francie said.

Latice made a sour face. "Would you? I mean, like, there's nothing to do. There's nobody cool here."

"Sandy's pretty nice," Francie ventured.

Latice rolled her eyes. "What a hick. Everybody around here is hicks."

Is a hick, Francie refrained from saying.

"Present company excluded, of course," Latice said, unconvincingly. "Can't even drive anywhere," she continued to complain. "No road! I suppose I could always drive the bulldozer."

"You've got a bulldozer?" Francie said.

"They brought it over on the ice in order to make the house and couldn't get it back, I guess. It's been here ever since."

"Where?" Francie asked, looking around.

"Back there." Latice waved her arm toward the back of the house. "At the end of the driveway."

"Driveway? What do you have a driveway for?"

"For when the road goes in." Latice rolled onto her belly, concluding the conversation. The sheen of the Coppertone oil reflecting off her back might be seen from outer space, Francie thought.

Back at her aunts' cabin, Francie threw off her shoes and ran into the lake with her shorts and T-shirt on.

Jeannette looked up from tinkering with the boat motor. "My goodness, you must be hot!"

"Hot and bothered," Francie said. She turned and floated on her back so she could talk to her aunt.

"Oh dear, that's not a good way to start a vacation." Jeannette looked concerned. "Maybe you'd like a cup of coffee and a roll?"

Francie groaned. "I'm stuffed! I've eaten so many bars, cookies, slices of pie, slabs of cake, and dishes of desserts that I should sink like a stone."

"Oh no, you won't sink. All that butter will help you float!"

Shoot, Francie thought, that's probably true. She *did* feel extra buoyant.

"Now, Frenchy," Astrid said. Where had she come from? Francie wondered. "When you talk to Buck, tell him we're ready to pass the cabin to you, but you don't want to keep it. You want to sell it. But you want us to live here as long as we'd like—until we die, if possible.

Francie scrambled to remember what Astrid was talking about—oh, yes, the real estate agent. She was supposed to set up an appointment with him.

"Am I even old enough to own property?"

"In this state? No. But Buck doesn't know how old you are, and that's all that matters for now."

Francie began to understand why her grandfather thought her aunts were a bad influence. "But why do you want to sell this place?" she asked.

"Oh, we don't want to sell it!" Astrid exclaimed. "Oh my, no! Not ever!"

"What is this about then?"

Ignoring her question, Jeannette said, "Just tell Buck you need the money for college."

"College!" Astrid said, "For the love of Mike! She's a detective! She doesn't go to college!"

"Well, what does she need money for then?" Jeannette asked.

"Wait! Wait!" Francie plowed her way out of the water. "What *is* this about me being a detective? Why does everybody keep saying I'm a—wait a minute! It's you! You two have been telling everyone I'm a detective. Why?"

"You were so convincing in your role on TV," Astrid said, handing Francie a beach towel.

Francie pressed the towel to her face and exhaled into it. This whole thing was insane. It was just insane. "I'm not a detective! I don't even *want* to be a detective! I'm an actor. That's what I want to be."

"That's nice, sweetie," Astrid said. "Now, when you talk to Buck, just make sure you let him know you need the money now—he doesn't need to know why you need money—but you'd like to know if there's a way we can live here until we pass away or can no longer stay here."

"Okay, okay, I get it," Francie said. She didn't, really, and was about to bring up the fact that she could maybe just *call* to set up an appointment, when suddenly she *did* get it. Sort of. She thought about the people she'd talked to that day who were selling their cabins. Ginger, Mrs. Smattering, Mrs. Hansen. They had all lost someone recently. Maybe her aunts were onto something. In any case, she wanted to talk to Sandy, so she'd go along with their scheme.

"Now, Frenchy, get out of those wet clothes and go to town," Jeannette said.

As Francie waddled in her wet clothes to the boathouse, her aunt shouted after her, "And while you're there, call your grandfather and tell him you're okay." She nodded her assent, but she had no intention of calling her grandfather and telling him anything.

7

A HEADACHE

FRANCIE DROVE HER AUNTS' BOAT across the lake where she found Sandy in the process of inspecting a boat.

"Inspecting it for what?" Francie asked when he was finished. "Drugs?" she joked.

"Plant life and stuff," he explained. "Invasives. Zebra mussels, mud snails, milfoil. Any one of those things could change this lake forever. Not in a good way."

Francie nodded. "Oh, yeah. I've heard about zebra mussels. Nasty things. So they're in lakes around here?"

"Yep," he said. "We're surrounded. Anybody wants to launch a boat here, it gets inspected."

"What if you find something?"

"Then they have to get the boat decontaminated. The DNR has a unit in Walpurgis."

Francie followed Sandy to the store where he took two bottles of soda out of the cooler, popped the caps, handed her one, and led her outside where they sat on the edge of a trampoline.

"I'm wondering," Francie mused, "do you think something sinister is going on over there?" She nodded her head toward the far shore.

Sandy took a swig of his Coke. "Don't know," he said. "What are you thinking?"

"It's my aunts," Francie said. "They think something fishy is going on. There have been so many deaths." She thought of telling him about the feeling of being followed but held back. She was less and less sure that had happened.

"People are getting old," Sandy said.

"That's what I said, too, but they're not dying of old age. They're dying in bizarre accidents. Did you hear about Warren?"

Sandy shook his head sadly. "Who'd have thought he would commit suicide?"

"My aunts don't think he did."

Sandy looked at her sideways. Even in a sideways glance, she could see his blue eyes shifting colors: pale blue, then turquoise, a flash of cobalt.

"What do they think?" he asked.

"I don't know exactly," Francie hedged a little. She didn't want to paint her aunts as any more kooky than people already thought they were, so she changed the subject. "Last night you mentioned that your dad died of a heart attack on a hunting trip."

Sandy stared at his Coke bottle.

"But you sounded like you weren't sure about that."

Sandy shrugged. "Yeah, I guess I did. I don't know why. Why shouldn't he die of a heart attack? People do. Must have had a bad heart."

The wind pushed the poplar branches around so that light fell on them in flickering bursts. Francie squinted against it; it seemed to aggravate the headache she felt coming on.

"You didn't know that he had a bad heart?" Francie asked.

Sandy shook his head. "He hadn't had any problems before."

"So, something doesn't seem right about it, does it?"

Sandy looked at her for a long moment, and she quickly said, "The thing is, when you said that, about your dad, I felt this twinge inside, because I've never believed my dad died accidentally, either."

"I thought it was a car accident."

Francie nodded. "It was. It just was never explained well enough, in my mind."

Sandy nodded and started to talk. "That's the way I feel, too. My dad went to his hunting shack with a bunch of buddies. I couldn't go—first time ever I didn't go along, but I was on the football team. So he went with a bunch of other guys."

"Who?" Francie asked, taking out her notebook.

"Just a minute," Sandy said.

He disappeared into a door that said "Office" and returned with a scrapbook. "Mom's a scrapbooker," he explained, paging through it. He pointed at a photo of two dead deer draped over the hood of a car. Standing nearby were three men in blaze orange hunting gear. Two of the men beamed wide smiles at the camera. The expression on Sandy Sr.'s face, however, looked more like one a deer throws at oncoming headlights.

"Those two look happy," Francie commented, "but look at your dad's face."

"I know," Sandy said. "It's not like him. It's one of the reasons I've always wondered about that whole event."

"Could he have been feeling ill then?"

"Yes, that's what others, including my mom, said: that he wasn't well. Anyway, neither of these guys would have wanted any harm to come to Dad—they were like brothers. This one here *is* his brother, in fact. They'd been fishing and hunting together for years, and they both wept like babies at the funeral—I'd never seen anything like it. That's why I don't really know why I think there was some kind of foul play, or whatever you call it. It's just a feeling."

"There wasn't an autopsy, I suppose," Francie said.

Sandy shook his head. "Naw. We're not really autopsy-type people."

"Sandy," Francie said, "there's one other person you've not mentioned."

"Who?"

"The person who took this picture. Who took it?"

Sandy blinked at her. "I don't know!"

"Where was the picture taken?"

"It was at the shack. You can see it there in the background."

"Was there another person along on the trip?"

"Nobody ever mentioned another person."

"Look at the shadow."

Sandy squinted at the picture. Once you knew what you were looking at, the shadow of a photographer was clear. "That's why you get paid the big bucks, right?" he said. "As a detective?"

"No!" she said. "I'm not a—"

Sandy's attention was diverted by a truck that pulled into the parking lot. A couple of guys got out and headed toward the store. Sandy got up to follow them in.

"Getting a load of potatoes?" Francie asked, nodding at the truck. The words "Northland Potatoes" were emblazoned on the side of it.

"What?" Sandy asked, turning back. Then, looking at the truck, he said, "No. Those guys are scouting the area for a big corporate potato growing operation. For McDonald's french fries, I guess."

"How do they expect to grow potatoes in the middle of a forest?"

"Oh, if they decide to plant potatoes, the forest has to go."

"Has to go?" Francie asked.

"They just remove it," Sandy said. "Fifteen hundred acres at a time. Apparently the sandy soil is what they want."

"Whoa," Francie said.

"Yeah," Sandy agreed. "Seems like everyone around here wants something other than forest from this forest."

Francie stared for a long while at the truck, thinking about what Sandy had said. Then she walked to her aunts' car, jingling the keys and supposing that if you were going to grow potatoes, you'd need a road to wherever it was you were going to plant them.

8

BUCK THORNE

The inside of Paradise Realty was a strange mix of carpeting, air conditioning, and rustic log furniture upholstered with bear motif fabrics. A fake stone fireplace loomed at one end of the reception area, with a large and real elk head presiding above the mantel.

The receptionist's nameplate identified her as *Darcee*.

"I'm looking for a real estate agent to, um, to tell me if I could..." Francie had no idea how to word this, but she told herself to pull it together and finished strong. "I have some property I'd like to sell on Enchantment Lake."

"Ooh, Enchantment! Buck'll be interested in *that*," Darcee said. She couldn't help staring at Francie's hair.

"I don't color it; it just grows that way," Francie answered Darcee's unasked question.

"Oh, huh!" Darcee said.

A young man rushed in through a back door, wearing a pair of swim trunks and flip-flops. He dashed through the office,

flinging open cupboard doors, rummaging through drawers, and slamming them shut.

Buck? Francie silently asked Darcee, mouthing the name.

Darcee shook her head and mouthed *Junior*. Then she swiveled her chair around to face the sunburned man whose hair, Francie noticed, was wet.

"Looking for loose change again?" Darcee asked astringently.

Francie turned away and tried to interest herself in a slick architect's drawing spread out on a desk. She had to look at it upside down, but it appeared to be a big development that included buildings, pools, tennis courts, and here and there a few little circular green things that were probably supposed to indicate trees. She concentrated on reading the big, block letters that were upside down, too, and made out "FIR Forest Development Enterprises." Right, Francie thought. I'll bet there's not one fir tree left by the time they're done. Like "Oak Ridge" with no oaks or "Birch Grove" without birch trees. Seems like everybody wants something other than forest from the forest, she remembered Sandy saying.

Darcee spun in her swivel chair, picked up the phone, and after the briefest of conversations, said to Francie, "Buck will meet you out at Enchantment."

Buck was a big guy, well over 200 pounds, wearing a western-style shirt with pearl snaps, brown polyester bootcut western-style pants, a belt with an enormous silver buckle, and cowboy boots. The boots were the oddest part of the outfit. As she watched Buck climb the stairs, Astrid wondered aloud if he didn't go "ass over teakettle" when he rode in aluminum boats.

"Now," Astrid said, "we're going to hide in the closet in the back room where we'll be able to hear."

"Hide? Why?" Francie asked.

"If Buck knows we're in on this idea, he might get suspicious," Jeannette said as they bustled off to the back room.

Buck came in, belly first. A toothpick danced around the side of his mouth while he surveyed the inside of the cabin. One mystery solved: this was definitely *not* the guy they were trying to set her up with. She sincerely hoped.

"I hear you're a big detective in New York" was the first thing out of his mouth.

She'd gotten used to hearing that statement, so rather than just being embarrassed about it, she watched his reaction to the idea.

He smirked an "I'm-not-afraid-of-you-little-missy" smirk. And yet, before the smirk fully settled in, a brief look of some complexity crossed his face. What did that look indicate? Perhaps if she really were a detective she would be able to interpret it, as TV detectives seemed able to do. As she pondered this, his face returned to its "little-missy" look.

"My aunts have gone to the neighbors for coffee, so we can talk frankly," she told him. "They would like to give this property to me, which is very generous of them, but I would like to sell it because I need the money." (What was she supposed to need the money for again?) "I need the money now, but is there any way my aunts would be able to stay on?"

"Oh, sure," Buck said. He offered to buy the property right away and allow the ladies to stay until they could no longer manage. Life estate, he called it. The price seemed reasonable. Somehow that made her even more suspicious.

"Awfully kind of you." Francie choked on the words. She had begun to understand her aunts' suspicions about Buck.

A loud crash followed by a series of small "thunks" issued forth from the back room. It sounded like a platter being dropped from a top shelf. Francie remembered that Astrid used to hide cakes and cookies when she and her brother were little so they wouldn't eat them all. Then she'd forget where they were. Francie pictured ancient bars scattered everywhere.

Buck's eyes narrowed. "Are you sure your aunts aren't here?" he said.

"Terrible mouse problem," Francie said. "Will I have to include that in the disclosure statement?" She wondered where she'd pulled the "disclosure statement" idea from.

"That's a mighty big mouse that can knock over a . . ."

"Squirrels?" Francie posited.

Buck shook his head and took a step toward Francie. She resisted the urge to step back and stood her ground.

"Raccoons," he hissed in her ear. "You don't want raccoons."

"Oh, gosh!" Francie exclaimed. "In the crawl space, maybe?"

"Yes, that's probably it."

"I'll get that taken care of right away," she said as she urged him toward the door.

"Your aunts are special people, you know," he said. "Kind of the matri-larks of the lake.

"Matriarchs?" Francie suggested.

"Yep," he said. "Can't imagine this shore without them."

Francie wondered if he was saying all this for her aunts' benefit because he knew very well they were hiding nearby. She suggested a look around at the property.

Stepping outside, Buck asked Francie what her aunts intended to do with their undeveloped property, the one on the other side of the Fredericksons'.

"I believe they intend to leave that to my brother."

"Uh-huh," Buck said. "And where is your brother these days?"

"I don't really know," Francie said. "Africa? Or maybe South America. Siberia? I can't keep track."

"Huh!" was Buck's response. "You likely to be speaking with him in the near future?"

"I doubt it," she said truthfully.

"How would a person get in touch with him?" Buck asked.

Francie shrugged. "Don't really know."

"So," Buck said, "shall I write up a purchase agreement for this property?"

Francie bit her lip, suddenly very nervous about all of this—about everything. She knew she was supposed to say yes to get the ball rolling. That's what her aunts wanted. But she was also afraid. Were her aunts putting themselves in danger on purpose? And what if somehow Francie accidentally really sold the place? She realized she couldn't bear the thought. "Let me think about it," she said. "I'm not sure what to do, but I'll make up my mind before I go back to New York."

Buck stuck a long grass stem in his mouth, looked at her sideways, and said, "Back to detective-ing?"

9
STRAWBERRY PICKING

"Well, Astrid, what do you think?" Jeannette asked as the three of them watched Buck's boat retreating across the lake.

"He's the one," Astrid said, her eyes glittering. The boat's wake rushed onto the shore, as if applauding.

"He's the one what?" Francie asked.

"He's the one who's been knocking off cabin owners around here. I suspect we're next," she said matter-of-factly. "Unless, of course, we do something about it first." She turned to Francie and smiled sweetly. "Let's go strawberry picking!"

Francie did not see how picking strawberries was going to stop Buck from doing anything, and she said so.

Astrid laughed her tiny, tinkling-bell giggle that always made Francie smile and said, "Of course not! But I definitely want to get enough strawberries for a pie."

"A pie!" Jeannette protested. "We'll never get that many strawberries!"

Francie didn't think so, either. The wild strawberries were so very, very tiny that you needed hundreds and hundreds of them to make a pie. But they were so very, very sweet and delicious, Francie's mouth started to water just thinking about them, so she said, "Let's see if we can!"

Their secret strawberry spot was on a sunny knoll overlooking the forest behind the cabin. From here it seemed as if the forest stretched forever. North and north into the great boreal forests of Canada. On days like this, when the wind blew from there, the smell of endless pines and lakes and granite filled the air. She felt herself snuffling the scent like a dog does, filling her lungs with it. It was a smell that called up some primal part of her, her wild, natural self. Her *real* self, she thought suddenly.

"Have you heard from your brother?" Jeannette was asking her.

"No," Francie said. "Not since . . . I can't remember, really. It was Christmas—"

"Oh! Christmas!" Astrid said.

"—a few years ago," Francie finished. The sight of a cluster of tiny red berries under the leaves suddenly made her feel close to tears.

"What happened between you two? You used to be so close," Astrid said.

"Close!" Francie exclaimed. "We fought like cats and dogs."

"That's what siblings who are close do," Astrid said. "Siblings who are not close don't have any reason to fight. What keeps the two of you apart?"

Francie dropped the few strawberries she'd found into her pail. They hit the bottom with the faintest *plink*. "I guess I don't really know," she said finally. "Somehow it's just become habit. It's just the way it is. We don't communicate. We're just so different," Francie said. "We don't have much in common."

Astrid snorted. "That's the most ridiculous thing I've ever heard!" she said. "You are like two peas in a pod."

"Ooh!" Jeannette squeaked. "Look at this spot!" She plunked herself down on the ground and went after the strawberries with a vengeance.

"How are we alike?" Francie protested. "He's a mostly penniless, mountain-climbing adventurer, and I'm a struggling actor who never leaves New York City."

"Yes, you do leave!" Astrid said. "You're here. And anyway, I'm not talking about what you *do*. I'm talking about who you *are*."

Francie grew very still, acutely feeling the breeze on her face. *My real self*, she thought again. What did that really mean? she wondered.

"You and your brother share a common fierce fearlessness, a kind of recklessness in the face of danger," Astrid went on. "You're both impulsive, high-minded, and nonmaterialistic. You are motivated by compassion."

"That's all true about him, maybe, but not me."

"Ha!" Astrid said.

"How can you say I'm fearless? When have I had to face danger? How can you say I'm motivated by compassion? I can't think of one compassionate thing I've done, unless you count donating a quarter for a newspaper from homeless people."

"Well, we know what we know," Jeannette sniffed. "Astrid, have you gotten any more berries?"

"Oh," Astrid said, "I've long ago given up looking for berries. Now I'm hunting for diamonds!"

That night, Francie happily and tiredly climbed into bed in the boathouse. The previous night with the wind chime and the strange noise and the footsteps all seemed as if it happened long ago or not at all. Her aunts assured her that nothing could possibly happen to them until Francie actually sold the cabin to Buck, because that wouldn't make any sense at all. Francie wasn't so sure about that, but she was happy to curl up alone with her thoughts and feelings.

So many feelings! Her anger and frustration had dissipated, and instead she was filled with gratitude. She was happy that she had this time with her beloved aunts. Her grandfather would say they had tricked her into coming. He would be at least disapproving and more likely furious. But what if they hadn't "tricked" her? Would she have come if they had just invited her? She was ashamed to admit that she probably wouldn't have; she was too busy with schoolwork and too broke, and there was always that next audition. How long might it have been before she'd come back here? It might have taken their actual deaths.

She thought about the feeling of the warm sun on her back when they'd been berry picking that afternoon. The lazy drone of a fly. The chickadees "chicka-dee-dee"-ing in the trees. Chatting amiably with her aunts, who seemed to know things about her that she didn't know. That feeling that she'd almost—almost—grasped who she really was. Was she fearless? Was she motivated by compassion? There was nothing to indicate that. It would be like her aunts to suggest that she was in case it might "take."

She was grateful to them. She didn't have a mother and a father to say kind things to her, and her grandfather didn't say kind things. Granddad, she thought. Had he found out where she'd gone? What was going on back in that world, that other world that seemed so distant now?

Well, she wouldn't worry about it. Tonight, she felt loved, and those feelings made a big warm circle around her. Still, it seemed that within the warm circle was a dark hole, endlessly deep. It was into this hole that she felt herself falling. Of course, that was mostly the reason she'd never come back. She was afraid to feel the pain of losing her father as keenly as she did here, at the lake, where everything reminded her of him. That warm sun on her back today made her ache a little bit inside. The lazy drone of the fly made her feel more acutely the drone of old pain. Those tender little birds, the chickadees—they were the fearless ones, so tiny, yet she'd seen them chasing blue jays, several times bigger than they were, away from their nests. Her father had tamed those little birds, putting birdseed on his hat and standing so still that they came and sat on his head and eventually his shoulders and even his hands. She carried an image in her mind of him this way, covered in chickadees. And now, seeing or hearing these birds caused her both little pricks of pain and somehow, mixed in, a kind of deep delight. A delight she was almost afraid to acknowledge.

She reached for the book on the bedside table and read from a poem by Wendell Berry:

When despair for the world grows in me
and I wake in the night at the least sound
In fear of what my life and my children's lives may be,
I go and lie down where the wood drake
rests in his beauty on the water, and the great heron feeds.
I come into the peace of wild things

She set the book down and listened, without thinking of anything else, to the raucous calls of loons on the lake. They cooed and hollered, yodeled, laughed crazily, sang with wild abandon. She could picture them, practically standing on the water with their big wings outstretched and flapping, a big Friday night dance. More coming in for landings, with long, slow approaches and the graceless splash as they touched down, the other loons gathering around to join the party.

Party. That party at the Fredericksons'—should she go? She pictured the partygoers gathering, preening, and squawking and laughing like loons, and Mrs. Frederickson would be in the midst of it all, making entrances like—oh, for the love of Mike!—Frederica Ricard! Star of screen and stage. As seen in film, television, on Broadway. Savery Frederickson was Frederica Ricard, Broadway star. *Former* Broadway star.

And she, Francesca Frye, was invited to her house for a party the very next night! Things might be working out very well, after all. Very well, indeed!

Francie blew out the lamp and laid her head on the deliciously soft pillow, closed her eyes, and fell asleep smiling.

10
SLEUTHING

AT THE ONE COFFEE SHOP IN TOWN, Francie ordered a "cappachino," as it was spelled on the menu, and sketched out the roadless side of the lake on a napkin, putting an X at every cabin where there was a suspicious death. Her list read:

Falling Tree Limb (Kevin Smattering)
Drowning (Mr. Hansen)
Snakebite (Mr. Simonsen)
Gunshot/Suicide? (Warren)
Poisoned Well (Ginger's dad)
Heart Attack? (Sandy's dad)

She resisted also writing:

Car Accident? (My dad)

Then she pulled out her laptop. In the time it took to drink her cappuccino, Francie found some interesting information. Of the causes of death, the snakebite was the weirdest one—until she found out that Mr. Simonsen had been a herpetologist.

Wasn't that someone who worked with snakes? Yes, according to Wikipedia.

How did people ever find out anything before Google?

But how might a well be poisoned? How might a falling tree branch not be an accident? That was harder to find.

On Buck Thorne's home page, she learned that he liked to fish for walleyes at night on Enchantment Lake. This didn't exactly hang him for Mr. Hansen's drowning, as there were probably hundreds of such fishing fanatics. But—what was this? A photo of Buck wearing blaze orange, holding up the head of a dead deer. "Buck's 15-point buck," the caption read. Although all guys in blaze orange jackets and hats looked alike to her, these particular guys looked familiar. Very familiar. Hadn't she just seen these same hunters in the photo Sandy showed her? She'd have to remember to have Sandy ask his uncle about it.

And then she learned that Buck had taken a community education course on snake and reptile identification. Well, well. There did seem to be a common thread, and if she were a detective—which she wasn't, she reminded herself and anyone else who might have been eavesdropping on her thoughts—her prime suspect, in whatever crimes might have occurred, if any crimes actually *had* occurred, would be Buck Thorne. For the love of Mike, as Aunt Jeannette liked to say, what a name!

She drained the dregs of her cappuccino and smacked her lips. In one afternoon of scrounging, she'd uncovered enough dirt on Buck to, if not hang him, at least seriously call him in for questioning—if she were an actual detective.

Maybe this "detective-ing" wasn't really all that hard.

On the way home, she thought about the party at the Fredericksons' that night. "What's the right thing to wear to a party like this?" she mumbled. "It doesn't matter, because for sure I don't have it." Painful irony! To leave New York to get your big break at a remote lake in northern Minnesota, and she had *nothing* to wear. She needed someone to help her. Ginger.

Ginger was sitting at her table, her head in one hand, her other hand wrapped around a glass of lemonade that Francie was pretty sure was spiked.

"You okay?" Francie asked.

Ginger sighed. "Yeah. No. I don't know. This thing with Warren. It's just too much with everything else that's happened. My mom and dad were in the middle of a divorce when Dad died. They were haggling over everything: money, property, including this place. Then this spring, when he died, the sheriff came out and made all kinds of insinuations about my mom—like she killed him! I feel bad for T.J. That's why I agreed to stay up here with him. So he could have one last summer at the lake. He and Dad were real close, and Warren had filled the gap a little bit. They were like soul mates, almost, Warren and T.J. Why would anyone kill him?"

"My aunts seem to think that someone is trying to scare people or wear them down to make them sell their property. If that's the case, who better to get rid of than Warren, the guy who makes it possible for these nice old ladies to stay in their cabins. And nice young ladies like you, I guess."

Ginger shivered. "That's creepy."

"Yeah," Francie agreed. She should probably feel a little creeped out about it too, but all she could really think about was getting to the party.

Ginger must have noticed her impatience because she glanced at her and said, "What's up with you?"

Francie explained that she was invited to the Fredericksons'. Ginger raised an eyebrow in response. "What I really need is something to wear," Francie said. "What do people wear to parties around here?"

"How should I know?" Ginger shrugged. "Do you think anybody invites anyone from the murdering Angell family to any-thing? And why do you want to go to the Fredericksons' anyway?"

"Don't you know who Savery is?"

"Sure. I met her at a potluck. Everybody was there, including your aunts. Who doesn't know Savery Frederickson?"

"Yes, but she's *not* Savery Frederickson! She's Frederica Ricard."

Ginger looked at her blankly.

"Star of stage and screen?"

"Really?" Ginger said. "I never heard of her."

"Well, mostly stage. And it was a while ago."

"Okay, so?"

"I'm an actor! I mean, I want to be," Francie said.

"Huh? I thought you were a detective."

"No! I've been trying to tell you!" Francie said. "My aunts start-ed that rumor—don't ask me why—and now everyone thinks I'm a detective, including Frederica. Mrs. Frederickson. Whatever her name is. But this party might be jam-packed with important theater people!" Francie rushed on, breathlessly. "Or maybe I can even get a chance to talk to Mrs. Frederickson. Uh, Frederica."

"Okay," Ginger said, "but you're missing a chance to stay here with me and play gin. And better yet, drink it. If you still want to go, you're welcome to have a look in my closet."

Ginger opened her closet to reveal a small selection of lake clothes and one simple black dress, which Francie chose. She didn't have quite the knock-out legs that Ginger had, but the dress fit well enough, and Ginger outfitted her with a simple necklace and earrings, too. "That should do it," she said. "You look smashing."

And definitely older than seventeen, Francie thought, eyeing herself in the mirror. Was that good? Or bad?

"Thanks a lot," Francie said. "If your light is still on later, I might stop by."

11
THE PARTY

THE PARTYGOERS were dressed in hues of watermelon and peach (or was it nectarine?). Plenty of gold jewelry created a dull gleam on the twilit deck. Francie, the only one in black, looked like she was on her way to a funeral. Circulating through the rooms, out onto decks and back inside, she caught snippets of conversations. A couple of men in sport coats were discussing "core samples" with two guys in jeans and T-shirts. Another man rattled on about "yields and commodity prices" with a woman who could barely suppress her yawns. Who were these people?

And where were the theater people? The impossibly thin people? The ratty sweaters? The tight black jeans? The sallow, spends-all-one's-time-in-a-dark-hole complexions?

"Hello, darlin'," Mrs. Frederickson said, sweeping up to Francie, looking classic and dramatic in a Grecian-style cerulean-blue dress and carrying a tray of canapés. "So nice of you to come. The kids are in the family room." She waved her free hand toward a stairway. "Downstairs."

"Mrs. Frederickson?" Francie began, intending to explain who she really was: an actor looking for work.

But Mrs. Frederickson turned away, wafting the tray of appetizers past Francie yet not close enough that she could actually nab one. "We were so drawn to the peace and quiet," she drawled to a woman nearby. "It was the kind of old-fashioned lake we found appealing. Real woodsy."

Francie looked out at the green sweep of lawn. A sprinkler chinged away at the far edge. "For liking it woodsy, you don't seem to have saved a lot of trees on your property," she mumbled.

"Well, they're so messy, aren't they?" the other woman said. Oops, Francie thought. Big mouth. "All those leaves and twigs and things," the woman went on. "You have to constantly pick up after them."

Francie wondered if this woman had any children or if she'd gotten rid of them, too, once she discovered they were messy.

A ruddy-faced man elbowed in to ask if she knew anybody looking to sell or if she herself was looking to get rid of some property. He was interested in buying around here.

"I don't own property," Francie answered.

"This young lady is not a landowner—*yet*," Mrs. Frederickson said. "She's a detective in New York."

"Actually—" Francie began, but all attention was at that moment diverted to a scene unfolding behind her. By the time Francie realized that people were not looking at her and turned to see what it was they *were* looking at, she caught the tail end of an argument that culminated with one of the many blonde women tossing a glass of something on someone. The someone, Francie noticed, was Buck.

"It's Rose," the lady next to her whispered to her husband. "Buck's ex-wife."

Rose *Thorne*? Francie thought. For the love of Pete, what a name!

Buck wiped down the front of his polo shirt, and Rose stalked out onto one of the many decks.

"Now, darlin'," Mrs. Frederickson said, turning once again to Francie, "the family room is down those stairs." She swept her elegant arm toward the stairway again, more insistently this time. "There'll be fireworks on the dock in a little while."

Francie dutifully walked downstairs into a scented cloud of perfume, aftershave, cologne, and hair product. Latice and her city friends were hanging out on couches and chairs, watching a movie and getting smashed. It looked like Latice had raided her parents' liquor cabinet for the hard stuff, while upstairs the adults sipped wine. One of the guys caught her eye—it was that guy she'd walked right into, the one with the bouquet of flowers, no doubt for a girlfriend, and yep, sure enough, he looked like he was with someone.

Except for that guy, and he seemed to be taken, these were not the people she was looking for, and at the first opportunity, Francie glided up the stairs and back into the tantalizing world of the adults.

The kitchen! Why hadn't she thought of it before? In her experience that was where actors hung out—close to the refrigerator.

The kitchen was strangely empty, further proving to her that there were no theater people here. The people at this party got enough to eat without scrounging in other people's kitchens, apparently.

She heard Buck's voice; he seemed to be coming her way. Having no desire to talk to him, she slipped into a pantry as he entered the kitchen. Buck turned on the tap and held a towel under it as another, younger man entered. Francie recognized him as Buck Jr.

"Hey, Pop," said the younger man.

"Oh, it's you, is it?" the elder Buck mumbled.

Francie took another step into the recesses of the pantry where, although she could no longer see, she also couldn't be seen. It made her feel detective-ish. Plus, she really didn't want to make small talk with either of them.

"I been looking all over for you," said the younger Buck.

"Yeah?"

"I need some cash."

"What else is new?"

"Come *on*."

"You know I don't have any cash."

"Everything tied up in real estate?"

"I'm warning you, Little Buck," Buck Sr. said.

"Don't call me that," Buck Jr. growled.

"Yeah, okay, whatever." That was Buck Sr.

"I thought you were gonna be selling condos like hotcakes by now."

"Yeah, well, I've run into a snag or two."

"Liquefy some assets, that's what I'm saying. My deal is gold—*gold*. You ever hear that old story about the treasure they say is buried around here?"

The treasure? Seriously? Francie leaned in.

Buck Sr. mumbled, bored.

"Well, Pop, I found it," Buck Jr. said. "It's in *there*."

Francie glanced around her, hoping he was not pointing at the pantry.

"That's not where it is," Buck Sr. said.

"Where is it, then?" said Junior.

There was the sound of ice clinking in a glass. Buck Sr. was the only person she'd noticed drinking a mixed drink. Everyone else was drinking wine or beer. That was a silly thing to think about when treasure was being discussed, Francie thought.

Buck Sr. grunted and swallowed.

"Where are the glasses?" young Buck asked. "I've got a power-ful thirst."

Francie heard his footsteps echoing around the immense kitchen, growing closer. She glanced up and noticed, through the glass windows of the cupboards in her hideout, glasses of every shape and size glittering inches from her nose.

"Try that pantry over there," Buck Sr. suggested.

12

FISHING

"Oh, never mind," Buck Jr. said, "I'll just have a beer."

Francie heard the fridge open, the clinking of glass, then the fizz of a bottle opening, followed by the ting of the cap on the counter. Then the click of heels on the tile floor, retreating. She resisted the impulse to heave a sigh and stepped out of the pantry into the kitchen.

"What were you doing in there?" Buck Sr. asked.

Oops. She should have counted the number of feet retreating. She'd have to remember that in future sleuthing situations.

"Me?" Francie squeaked. "Looking for a glass."

"Couldn't find one?" Buck said, nodding toward her empty hands.

"They all looked too nice," she answered. "I just wanted an ordinary glass—like you've got. She nodded at the glass in his hand, filled with ice. "You know, for a glass of water."

Buck took a tumbler out of a cupboard and filled it with water from the tap, then handed it to her and grunted. "Made a decision about that property yet?" he asked casually, but his stare was intense, his eyes moist with drunkenness or desperation—Francie couldn't tell. She knew what her aunts wanted her to do—say "yes!" But she couldn't.

"Soon," she said. "Just checking on a few things."

He opened his mouth, then closed it. Then again. It made her think of a Finnish folk story about why fish do that: they *think* they're talking, but since they're underwater, they can't hear, so they just go through the motions, and it seems like talking to them.

"Listen," he said, suddenly sounding very drunk. "Lez go fishin'." He flung an arm around her.

"Sure, Buck, I'll go fishing with you sometime," she said, uncoiling his arm from her shoulder. "In a few days maybe." He didn't know that in a few days she planned to be gone.

"No," Buck said. "I think we should go right now."

"I just got here!" she protested.

"Nothin' going on here," he said. "Come on, lez go." He grabbed her arm and steered her through the kitchen, down a set of stairs, in and out of several rooms. Francie craned her neck to look at the *Architectural Digest*–worthy furnishings, art, and flower arrangements. Wow! Frederica had made some solid money. Or the money was courtesy of her husband, Francie supposed. Who knew what business he was in?

Finally, while crossing a series of decks, Francie started to get nervous. Buck had not gotten distracted or changed his mind through all those rooms. He was still dragging her toward the dock.

She did not want to go with him. Probably not ever, but for sure not right now. She still hadn't met the theater people. There were bound to be some at this party somewhere.

"I wanna tell you somethin'," he said. "I think you'll be extra in'erested in it. You being a detective and all."

Argh! He *would* dangle that enticing tidbit in front of her. Although he really was too drunk to drive a boat.

"All right," she said, "if I can drive the boat."

"Alrighty," he said, "*if* you can drive the boat, you can drive the boat." He laughed at his joke.

"Which one's yours?" she asked, surveying the jumble of boats and the big pontoon tied to the dock. She intended to get in first and start it before he could. Somehow, he was at the motor by the time she climbed in. He pulled the starter cord a few times, revved the motor, and they were off. Why was he driving an ordinary fishing boat, she wondered. Didn't he have a big speedboat parked at Sandy's?

As if reading her thoughts, he said, "Buck Jr. took the big rig somewhere. This here one is better for trolling anyways."

It was the tail end of twilight. Just the two of them in the boat, exactly like in *The Godfather* when Al Pacino or whoever it was took Freddy out in the rowboat. She would be the Freddy character, she thought glumly, or was it Fredo? Anyway, the one who doesn't come back.

She looked longingly at the shore, rapidly becoming a dark smudge. You could tell where the Fredericksons' house was, though—the place looked like a cruise ship run aground. Electricity, she thought. They had it.

Buck cut the motor and offered to bait her hook. She took him up on it—since the bait was leeches—and she cast her line into the dark purple water.

They fished in silence for a while, then suddenly he said, "You lie, right?"

"I beg your pardon?" Francie asked.

"I mean, as a detective. I seen them shows. Them detectives are always lying in order to get a confession or whatever. So, do you?"

Francie swallowed. What was the right answer to that question? Of course, she was lying right now by pretending to be a detective. She didn't see any reason to tell him the truth. "I guess you could call it that, but we prefer the term 'professional discretion.'"

"Profezzional discrezion," he repeated. "I like that." He was silent for a moment, and Francie listened to the waves nudging the boat, pushing them toward shore. That gave her some comfort. The sooner they got to shore, the sooner she could get out of this boat and get back to meeting the right people.

"Well, then, I guess you know how it can happen," he was saying. "You tell just a little white lie and then another and pretty soon you're pretty good at it. Easy to lie when you're in real estate. Job almost requires it; it's just a matter of how *much* are you gonna lie, ya know? Where's the line going to be? Them detective shows . . . telling little white lies . . . catch the culprit . . . figure you know what I'm talking about," Buck finished.

"What?" she said. What had he just said? She'd been thinking how best to approach Mrs. Frederickson.

"Are you Catholic?" Buck asked.

Francie shook her head.

"Well, in Catholicism there are sins of commission and sins of omission. Things you do and things you don't do, things you say and things you don't say. You might just not say something. That's omission. Just don't mention that a house has had water in its basement, you know? It will probably never happen again anyway. That sort of thing. Not what you'd even call a lie." He jigged his line a bit.

"What *would* be a lie?" Francie imitated his jigging style.

Buck didn't say anything and Francie took a moment to reel in her line and check her bait. "Do you think they've been nibbling at this?" she asked, dangling the leech in front of Buck.

"Does it feel like they're nibbling at it?"

"I guess not," she said, and threw her line back in the water. "What would be a sin of—what was that other kind of lie?"

"Commission," Buck said. "That might be something like mis-showing where the property line is. There are lots of ways to lie a little bit, without it seeming like lying."

"Uh-huh," Francie said. She shivered involuntarily.

"Cold?" Buck said. "I have a jacket you can wear."

"Uh, okay," Francie said. She wasn't cold; she was scared of where this conversation was going. Good thing it was dark so that he couldn't see her face, she thought. Even though she was frightened of what she was about to say, she heard it coming out of her mouth anyway. "It sure seems odd," Francie said, trying to sound casual, "how many accidental deaths there've been out here."

"It's a very dangerous place, out here, without a road," Buck said. "No way to get to a hospital quick, not even anywhere a helicopter could land."

The Fredericksons' expanse of lawn flickered through Francie's mind, and she wondered if important, busy, influential Hollywood people came and went that way. "You've been buying cabins along this shore," she went on, as firmly and calmly as she could, "and agreeing to allow the inhabitants to live in them as long as they'd like to—"

"Life estate, it's called," Buck said. "It's perfectly legal, if that's what you're wondering. Now, I know it's hard for you to accept," he went on, "but these people are getting old, Francie; naturally they're going to start dying."

"But they're not dying from old age, Buck. They're dying from weird accidents. There are so many of these accidents that they start seeming suspicious to the casual outsider." Casual outsider? Had she just said that? What was that supposed to mean?

"That's just the police lady in you thinking that." He said that rather derisively, she thought, as he stumbled on. "And if a person *did* off a few of these old people, who would blame him, really? There's such a thing as progress, you know. But these people don't seem to know it, with their cobwebby little places, full of carpenter ants and mildew. There could be brand-new million-dollar places along here, you know."

"And that would be good?"

"That'd be good for all the people who'd like a nice place to live that doesn't take a day and a half to get to by boat—what a hassle!"

"You know a lot of these people?"

"*Those* people!" He nodded at the party house. "They all want a place here, on this side of the lake."

"They do?" Francie looked longingly back at the party house. "What do they like about it?"

"It's unspoiled!"

"Well, wouldn't putting condos up and a road in, uh, spoil it?"

"Spoil it? It would make it ac-ces-si-ble!" he said, as if she might not understand the word. "Accessibility doesn't spoil anything. It just makes the unspoiled places accessible."

"What *does* spoil a place?"

"Sour old people," he said grumpily.

"So have you been getting rid of some of those sour old people? It seems like some of them are people whose cabins you've purchased." She couldn't believe that came out of her mouth, but there it was, plopped out in the boat as if it were a fish on the end of the line.

He seemed to stare at it for a while, there at the bottom of the boat, then said, "Now, wait a minute. I never said I killed anybody. Some people have basically killed themselves through their own carelessness or stupidity. I don't see that it's my fault."

A burst of fireworks went off on the other side of the lake, twinkling brilliantly against the now dark sky, followed a few moments later by a series of pops and bangs. Francie remembered that Mrs. Frederickson had said they were going to shoot off fireworks on the dock later. She hoped she lived to see it.

"I'm not in the habit of poisoning wells, you know," Buck was saying, when she tuned back in. "A guy could do it, though, just enough to make someone sick, if he knew the right amounts."

Wait. What? What had Buck just said? "A guy could poison a well?" Francie repeated. "Could a guy make a tree branch fall down and kill someone?"

"That's what I'm talking about!" Buck cried. "What kind of person would go to sleep in a room with a big tree branch dangling by a shred over the roof? Wouldn't you think they'd check? Who'd think a branch like that would crash through the roof? You'd think it would just put a dent in it."

Francie shook her head as if she couldn't believe the stupidity of some people. "And the water moccasin? Speaking hypothetically, of course. How would a guy come up with an idea like that?" God, she prayed, what *am* I doing?

"Again proving the stupidity of people. You'd think a herpiologist—"

"Herpetologist?" Francie asked. "A person who studies snakes?"

"Yeah, that's what that Simonsen fellow was. He had crates full of them things. Frankly, the whole area is safer without them snakes around."

I'm a pretty good swimmer, she thought. If he just throws me in, I can make it—as long as I can get out of this ridiculous jacket. She knew she should say something and found herself talking like her detective character. "You were out in the boat with Wally Hansen the night he drowned, too, weren't you?" she asked.

He gave her a sidelong glance. She hoped he couldn't tell that under his warm jacket, she was shaking. What would my TV detective character ask right now, she wondered. Then she knew, but thought, *oh God, this is the one that'll get me thrown overboard.* "I've got one more question," she said, "about Warren."

Buck busied himself with his tackle box. "Now you're just crazy," he muttered, but he seemed noticeably more nervous, all darting eyes and licking lips. "I'll tell you one thing," he said finally. "You're barking up the wrong tree." He snapped the box shut, sat up, and said, "Here's something I do know about. Something that happened a long time ago—"

Francie's insides turned to water—a lake filled with schools of swarming minnows, swarming and swimming, jostling and bumping into each other. Somehow, she knew what he was going to say before he said it.

"—having to do with your parents," he finished.

The minnows jolted to a halt. Then sloshed back and forth, back and forth, waiting.

"I can tell you something about your mother," he said.

Their eyes met. In the dark, his eyes glistened like something amphibious. Francie glanced away, her gaze resting on Buck's tackle box.

Maybe her heart was not kept inside a pretty silver box somewhere, she thought, but instead inside a battered plastic box, tangled in monofilament and pierced with spinner and daredevil hooks.

No! she thought. She didn't want to hear anything from him. This was not the way it was supposed to happen! This was not the way she had envisioned hearing about her mother. Somehow it didn't seem like it would be anything good, coming from him.

Still, nobody else had ever offered any information. Shouldn't she at least find out what it was?

"What do you—" she started to say, but there was a sharp

yank on her line, and her fishing rod bent over, twitching. She gripped the rod with both hands.

"Reel it in!" Buck barked.

"Definitely a fish," she said. "It's not the bottom." She could feel the fish struggling on the other end, then diving. The reel made a groaning click with each turn.

"Must be a lunker," Buck said, scrambling around in the dark for the landing net. "You got it okay?"

"Yeah," she said through gritted teeth.

"It'll hold." he said, "That's 30-pound test line."

She reeled and reeled, it felt like forever, then suddenly saw the thing, a big walleye, rise just below the surface, its dusky side gleaming like pewter.

"Bring it closer to me," Buck said. "Bring it over here."

"No!" she said. "You bring the net over here!"

Buck leaned over to snag the fish, but his boots went out from under him and the net dropped into the lake. Momentarily startled, Francie let up on the tension and the fish swam free, giving a flip of its tail and then diving back to the black depths.

"Dang!" Buck said.

"Get your net at least," Francie said, reeling in her line.

Buck reached out for the landing net, but boat and net were quickly separated as the boat drifted away. He scrambled back to start the motor, grunting as he pulled at the starter.

Voices drifted out over the water from the party. The voices had grown louder, and there were peals of brassy laughter, then a series of splashes accompanied by squeals and shrieks. It sounded like the young people's party had moved outside and off the end of the dock.

She reeled in her line, secured it with its now-empty hook, and was just setting the rod down when a movement by the side of the boat made her jump. A dark shape lunged from the water, as if the fish were coming for her. She yelped, then saw it was the head of a person. It was that guy—the same guy she'd glimpsed in Fredericksons' family room. He raised his glistening and— she couldn't help but notice—nicely muscled arm, holding the net in his hand like a trident, like one of those gorgeous Greek gods. Neptune, maybe. Or was Neptune a Roman god?

"Lose something?" he said, dropping the net into the boat.

Francie, having lost her breath, was unable to respond audibly.

The motor kicked in, and Buck yelled, "Hey, kid! Watch out!"

Buck steered for the dock while the young god swam backward out of the way and disappeared into the darkness.

13

GO DARK

AFTER HER ENCOUNTER WITH BUCK, Francie was too frazzled to even think of making a good impression on anybody, so she stumbled along the path toward home. In the dark. She had a flashlight, but she felt weirdly safer with it off, as if the light would make her a target.

Lines from one of the poems in the book on her nightstand came to her: *To go in the dark with a light is to know the light. To know the dark, go dark.*

She marveled at how her eyes could adjust to the nighttime darkness. There were still occasional fireworks twinkling across the lake, and the party house behind her was lit up like Times Square, but here, in front of her, the forest was draped in black velvet, and moonlight sparkled on the ground like lost jewelry—a gold necklace, a spangly bracelet, an expensive watch, its face glinting among the needles.

She let her feet feel their way and imagined the evening's experiences as a kind of white mist rolling off her back. What a strange night! She'd been so full of excitement and hope going

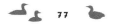

in—maybe a big break waiting for her or at least a possible connection. That had been a bust.

Then out of the blue Buck had brought up her mother, had
said he knew something about her. Why hadn't Francie pressed
him on that question? Wasn't that what she wanted above all
else, information about her mother? But it wasn't supposed to
happen that way, like it was some kind of shady drug deal.

She supposed her father would have told her something
eventually, but he died too soon, before she was old enough. Old
enough for what? she wondered. Why did she have to be "old
enough"? What *was* it about her mother that was so bad that no
one would tell her? That had to be it, didn't it? Her mother must
have been bad, and that's why her father had never been willing
to tell her anything. Maybe that was why she didn't press Buck
for more information. Maybe she was just too afraid to find out.

She felt herself sinking into a gloomy hole, full of murky
thoughts and nameless fear. Then, eerily, the feeling within her
seemed to take on an actual shape, a shape that moved ahead of
her, appearing then disappearing between the trees.

The shape, she quickly realized, was not her imaginary fear
or the "big question" moving about in the trees; it was an actual creature. Her stomach lurched. She tried to remember what
you were supposed to do to protect yourself in these situations:
Don't run! (That makes you look like prey.) *Make yourself look really big.* (That's what you're supposed to do in the case of mountain lions.)

She bent down and picked up a big stick and raised her arm.

The creature rushed out of the trees and lunged toward her,
snatched the branch out of her hand, and sat down in front of
her, panting.

"Rusty," she sighed.

Rusty wagged his tail, balancing the long stick in his mouth
like a tightrope walker's pole.

"Sorry. No fetch," Francie said. "Come on, let's go."

The dog jogged along in front of her. The stick in his mouth was just a little too long to fit crosswise in the path, so he kept getting hung up when the two ends of it jammed behind trees on either side, stopping him cold.

This made her laugh, and by the time they came out of the woods into Ginger's yard, her breathing had fallen back into a more normal pattern.

The cabin was dark, and Francie wondered if she should knock or just open the door and let the dog in. Was Rusty supposed to be inside at night? And why would you name a black dog "Rusty"?

She reached for the latch, then stopped, feeling the back of her neck prickle. She sensed someone behind her.

Francie whirled around to face Ginger. They both yelped.

"Ginger!" Francie gasped. "What—?"

Ginger held up her hand and said, "Sorry I startled you."

"You *and* your dog! Oh, is that why you're out at this hour? Looking for your dog?"

"Oh . . . yeah," Ginger said. "He's why I was out. I was looking for him. Rusty, come here," she scolded.

Rusty trotted over to her, staying just out of her reach.

"Want to come in for a nightcap?" Ginger asked, somewhat unenthusiastically.

"No, thanks," Francie said. She suddenly felt chilled and inexplicably afraid. She said good-bye and continued down the path.

She was almost home when it occurred to her to wonder why Ginger hadn't been calling for the dog if she'd been looking for him. Francie hadn't heard anything. She had the distinct feeling that Ginger was lying. Why? What had she been doing out there in the woods?

Tomorrow she would ask her. If she dared.

14

THE PUZZLE

THE NEXT MORNING, Francie found Jeannette sitting at the table by the picture window, working on a jigsaw puzzle.

Francie sat down next to her and fiddled with a puzzle piece. "Where's the picture?" she asked.

"The picture of what, Frenchy?" her aunt said.

"The picture on the box of what the puzzle is supposed to look like."

"Oh, we don't use that," Jeannette said. "We've done these same puzzles so many times, we had to find a way to make it more challenging. So we don't use the picture."

"But all these puzzle pieces are the same color! They're all blue! How can you possibly do this puzzle without the picture?" Francie thumbed a piece while trying to discern what the image could possibly be. "It's impossible," she grumbled.

"You seem out of sorts today, sweetheart," Jeannette said. "Was the party a disappointment?"

"It was strange," Francie admitted, "that's for sure." She

thought about her conversation with Buck, his possible confession, and all the strange deaths they'd talked about the previous night.

She'd had a morbid fascination with accidental deaths ever since she was ten years old. It had to do with her father's own accident, also unsolved—in her mind, anyway. It's why she'd felt a jolt when Sandy said his dad's death was suspicious. She'd always thought that, too, about her own father, although the report said it was a "vehicular accident." She had read the report so thoroughly the paper was worn thin, some of the words rubbed out. It had simply said he had "lost control" of the car on a wet, curving road along the Pacific Coast near Big Sur and plunged over a cliff.

The part she wanted filled in was *why?* Her father had not been the type to lose control of a car. He'd driven in countries with sketchy traffic laws all over the world: Ghana, Italy, Bolivia, Tibet. And he loses control on a quiet evening in California?

Her grandfather had said, when she had endlessly pestered him with this question, that perhaps an animal jumped out and he swerved to avoid it. Never swerve to avoid an animal, have I told you that? Yes, Grandad, you have, and you also always told Dad that, which is why I don't think he would've swerved to avoid an animal.

Perhaps a pedestrian then, he'd said.

There's no mention of a pedestrian in the report.

Maybe he hit a slippery spot in the road.

The whole road was slippery!

That's the way the conversation went, and perhaps that kind of questioning was why her aunts thought she should be a detective.

But she had never solved that mystery, nor had she solved the huge, looming mystery of her life, the one she was never able to get answers to, the one she had stopped even asking about: her mother, about whom she knew nothing. How was it possible not to know anything about one's mother?

She had a friend who didn't know who her father was—that was plausible. She also had a friend who was adopted and didn't know who her biological mother was—but they still had mothers! How could you not know anything about your own mother? All Francie knew was that her mother was dead and had been for a long time.

Francie had learned to stop asking. Her grandfather would say nothing; her aunts murmured little placating nothingisms; her own father had put her off. "I'm sure he meant to tell you all about her when you'd gotten a little older," her aunts had told her when she peppered them with questions. But then he died and that put an end to everything.

But how could you know who you were—or who you were supposed to be—if you didn't know your own mother? Maybe that was why she was drawn to acting: she could try on different skins, different characters and personae. Maybe one of them would feel right, and then she'd have a better idea of who she was.

"Frenchy?" Jeannette said. "Is that all you have to say about the party? That it was strange?"

"Oh!" Francie flinched, then refocused. Glancing at the puzzle, she noticed that while she'd been ruminating her aunt had managed to fill in a large section.

"The whole thing was a bit surreal," she said. "There was an odd assortment of people there, but the strangest one of all was Buck. He seemed nervous, edgy. Well, you would be, wouldn't you, if you were confessing to more or less killing people?"

"He *confessed*?" Jeannette exclaimed.

Had he? Now Francie wondered. What *had* he said? She'd

been distracted, strategizing about who to talk to at the party and wondering whether she'd come back alive from the fishing trip, and then she had been distracted by the Greek god in the lake.

"It's hard to say, really. I wish I had been secretly recording our conversation so I could listen to it again. It sure seemed like he was confessing to, if not murder, then whatever almost-murder is."

"Manslaughter?" Jeannette suggested.

"Maybe," Francie said.

Had he really confessed? But why would he confess to *her*? And then on top of it, he'd dropped the bombshell that he knew something about her mother.

"So if he really confessed," Jeannette said, "perhaps you should go to the police."

Should she? But then she might never find out what Buck knew about her mother. "No!" Francie said, a little too forcefully, so she added, "Not yet." Quickly changing the subject, she asked, "Why do you think the deaths have something to do with the road? It seems to me to have more to do with the acquisition of property." She wondered if she should tell her aunts that she suspected Mrs. Hansen and Mrs. Smattering had signed their places over to Buck. And the Angells were selling, too.

"Well, perhaps you're right," Jeannette said. "Astrid is the one who's so convinced it's about the road. But you know, once the properties are sold, there will be more pressure than ever to get a road, since the folks who like it the way it is will be mostly gone."

"Except for us, of course," Astrid said, coming out from the kitchen with a batch of cinnamon rolls. "And we're the crucial ones."

If it *was* about a road, her aunts would be under a lot of pressure, since they owned the two properties on each end of the roadless area. She felt queasy just thinking of what it could mean if Buck really had been arranging fatal accidents for people he wanted to get rid of. Perhaps Astrid had been right when she'd said earlier that they were "the prime victims."

"Where are they planning to put the road, anyway?" Francie asked.

"Oh, back there, behind the cabins," Jeannette said. "Right through the old peat bog."

There *was* an old bog back there, Francie remembered. She and her brother had loved to go there to look for pitcher plants after they learned that the plants were carnivorous. They had spent a lot of time in that bog one summer.

"Doesn't that count as wetlands?" Francie asked. "And wouldn't that qualify the area for protection?"

"I don't know. That bog is so old, there's quite a bit of it that's not wet anymore. Probably some pretty prime peat, though. I'm surprised someone isn't digging it up and selling it to Home Depot."

Francie sat back in her chair and stared out the window at the lake. Maybe the puzzle picture was of a lake. That would explain why it was all blue. The lake she could see outside the window was not blue at all, but an eerie green, and farther out there were gray patches and almost-black patches where the sun was obscured by clouds. An island about a half-mile out was alternately bright with sun or cast into dark shadow by the shifting clouds.

This whole mystery was a big puzzle, Francie thought, one that she was as incapable of solving as she was of finding a place for this one puzzle piece she'd been holding all this time. As for the mystery, things seemed as if they should be fitting into place, but somehow— "Something is wrong," she said out loud. "But I don't know what it is."

"Well," Astrid said, staring out at the lake with her. "One thing that's wrong is that island is getting smaller."

Jeannette snorted, and that made Francie start to giggle, and soon they were all guffawing like adolescents. She suddenly felt like the grown-up of the three of them. Along with that came a feeling of responsibility toward them.

Francie put down her puzzle piece, got up, and hugged them both. "I have to go to town," she said. "There's something I need to do."

15

THE SHERIFF'S OFFICE

THE SHERIFF LEANED BACK in his swivel chair and laughed. "He told you *what*? He said *what*?" He laughed so hard he started wheezing. "Listen, little missy, I know Buck. We went to high school together; we go elk hunting in Montana together every year." He nodded with his head to the big rack of antlers mounted on the wall over his desk. "Buck ain't no murderer." He leaned over and scratched his dog—a black lab—behind the ears.

"He doesn't seem to have any trouble killing elk," she muttered.

"What's that?"

Francie eyed the rack. "What kind of a gun do you have to have to kill one of those things?" she asked.

"Well, me personally, I use a 30.06. Some others use a—now wait a minute. I know what you're thinking, but you're off the track. Warren shot himself with his own 20-gauge shotgun, same gun he uses for grouse."

"What makes you so sure it was a suicide?" Francie asked.

"'Cuz he shot himself?" the sheriff said, with not a little sarcasm.

"What makes you so sure about that?"

"He left a note." He shoved a scrap of paper at her. "I'm sorry, but I have to," it said.

"That's a suicide note?"

"It was found right by the body."

"'I have to'—that could mean anything!" Francie said.

"It *could*," the sheriff said, "but in this case, it was found right next to his body. 'I have to' followed by a period. Maybe that's all he had to say."

"It's so vague. Why wasn't he more specific?"

"Like 'I'm sorry, but I have to shoot myself in the head'?"

"I don't know—it just could mean anything. 'Sorry, I have to go to town. Back soon.' 'Sorry, I have to bail the boat.' 'Sorry, I have to run over to Ginger's to fix her pump,' which is what he told her he was going to do yesterday."

"Warren was a man of few words."

"Obviously. But was he also a man of no punctuation? Look: that's not a period, that's a blood spatter. See? Look at the reverse of the page. There's no indentation. *And*, he didn't sign it."

"Looks like a suicide note to me." The sheriff leaned back in his chair and crossed his arms across his belly.

"Do you have a superior?"

"I don't know how it works out there in the Big Apple, but in this here Little Apple, I *am* the superior."

"I suppose you think all those deaths that have happened in the last year out on Enchantment have been accidental."

"This is the wild northwoods, miss; things happen."

"Do things like that happen on other lakes around here?"

"Sure. Some."

"Numbers? Numbers of suspicious deaths in numbers of years?"

"I don't have time to keep count. Right now there's a lot of stuff happening in town. There's a fishing contest, a historical society conference . . ."

"Historical society—that means a lot of drunken, late-night knife fights?" Francie said.

"Anyway, who says the deaths are suspicious?" the sheriff went on, ignoring Francie's sarcasm. He stood up and poured himself a cup of sour-smelling coffee. "I thought you were supposed to be on vacation from your detective job."

Oh, crikey, Francie thought, even *he* thinks I'm a detective. "Listen," Francie said, ignoring that, "I'm just concerned for the people of Enchantment. It seems really creepy how many weird deaths there are, and last night Buck all but confessed to arranging accidents for people. He said he never meant to kill anyone; they were just accidents that went awry, according to him, so your theory about him not being a cold-blooded killer is perhaps correct—until now, until Warren."

The sheriff sighed and rubbed his head. "I think Buck drank too much and was yankin' your chain."

Francie gave him the *look*.

"Okay, okay, tell you what," the sheriff said. "I'll have a little chat with him."

"No!" Francie cried. "You have to bring him in and hold him. If you won't investigate, then I will. I'll bring you enough proof. I'll find it and bring it in. Just keep him here before he can kill anyone else." For a moment, she felt like she was back in her show. She almost remembered the stage directions for that little speech.

"There's such a thing as jurisdiction, you know," the sheriff said.

"If you tell him I talked to you, I might be the next victim."

"Don't you think you're being a little paranoid? Listen here, now. I know how to use the innernet. I don't see where your name is listed as a detective anywhere."

Suddenly something kicked in. Francie had trained as an actor; why not use it? The sheriff was treating her like a kid, and so would everyone else if they knew she wasn't really a detective. If everybody thought she was a detective, and being a detective could get her somewhere, why not use it? She put her hands on his desk and leaned toward him. "Do you really think the NYPD would put my name and picture up on their website if I am going to be an effective undercover cop? I don't know how it works here in this *Little Apple*, but out there, in the *Big Apple*, we don't broadcast that we're undercover cops. Kinda defeats the purpose, you know what I'm saying? Now *you* listen. If I turn up dead in your *jurisdiction*, Sheriff—" (here she made a show of reading the nameplate on his desk) "*Rydell Johnson*, you'll have the whole NYPD to answer to."

That would give him something to chew on. "Now excuse me. Since you don't seem inclined to take care of your own criminals, I've got a lot of work to do."

It was a bit over the top—like something on a TV cop show. Perfect.

16

BABYSITTING

NOW WHAT?

First, she canceled her flight. There was no way she was going to leave her aunts alone now. What she *was* going to do, she wasn't sure, but she knew she had to stay. Maybe she could still connect with Mrs. Frederickson. And if things settled down in the next few days, she might be able to get back to New York in time for the next audition.

She checked her phone. Augh! An urgent message from Granddad: "Francesca, call ASAP. Need to talk." She felt a twinge of guilt and another of anxiety but tossed the phone into her backpack. She'd deal with him later.

The rest of the afternoon, she ran a few errands for her aunts, then went into the coffee shop, flipped open her laptop, and mulled. Obviously, she was going to have to find proof of Buck's guilt herself. And fast, before any other people were "accidentally" killed. But how?

There must be a way of digging up some dirt on Buck. Then

again, what if it wasn't Buck? The sheriff certainly didn't think so. And when she thought about it, Buck did not strike her as being smart enough or patient enough to orchestrate a string of murders. Still, he was the constant in all of these unusual deaths, or most of them, anyway. Perhaps he was smarter than he pretended to be. That would be something a very clever person could do. She had an actor friend who was one of the smartest people she knew, but he had a steady job on a sitcom playing an ignoramus. "The smart actors play dumb characters better than dumb actors do," a director had told her once, when she'd squeaked about getting the dumb blonde part (for which she had to wear a wig, of course). That shut her up. So she ought to know better than to make such assumptions.

Since she couldn't come up with any great ideas about how to investigate Buck or how to respond to her grandfather's phone message, she decided to go back to the cabin.

On Francie's way up to the cabin from the lake, Ginger intercepted her to ask if she'd mind babysitting T.J. for the evening. She was going out for dinner, she said.

"A date?" Francie asked.

"Don't act so surprised. I'm not that bad looking," Ginger said.

"I didn't mean that," Francie explained. "I mean, who is there to date around here?" The gorgeous Greek god of the previous night flickered through her mind, but she didn't even know who he was, so she couldn't ask. "Sandy?" she said.

"God, no!" Ginger said. "Stop asking. I'm not going to tell you."

"Not Buck Jr.," Francie guessed. "Please say no."

Ginger laughed. "No."

"Good," Francie said. "Who then?"

"I told you, I'm not going to tell you!" Ginger protested.

"What? Why? Are you serious?"

Ginger laughed and flipped her hair off her face and trip-tropped down the path. "I'll send T.J. over shortly, okay?" she called over her shoulder.

"Yeah, okay," Francie answered. "I'll try to get the aunts to cook something normal. What does he like to eat, by the way?"

"Anything! The weirder the better!" Ginger shouted back, laughing.

"That's lucky!" Francie called back.

Ginger seemed really happy. That was nice. She deserved something nice, Francie supposed, although she wondered if Ginger's mother would approve of her dating while she was supposed to be babysitting her little brother.

At dinner Francie played with her mashed potatoes, fwapping them with the back of her spoon. Why wouldn't Ginger tell her who she was going out with? Francie swirled her potatoes slower. Was she *really* on a date? Why had she been out when Francie had come by after the party? Had it been Ginger who had been lurking when Francie had gone out to silence the wind chime? Though the evening was warm, a shiver ran up her arms.

She turned and looked at T.J., who was busy smashing his peas deep into his potatoes. He was distracted, too. He acted uncomfortable. Afraid, even.

"Is there something wrong with the potatoes?" Astrid said sharply. "For the love of Pete! A couple of disagreeable porcupines would be better company than you two."

"Sorry," Francie said. "Just thinking." She shoved her potatoes into the shape of a volcano.

Astrid went into the kitchen, and Francie turned to T.J.

"So, T.J.," she said, "where did Ginger go tonight?"

T.J. lifted one shoulder in a shrug. "Dunno," he said.

"Who's her date?"

T.J. lifted his other shoulder. "Dunno. She didn't tell me."

"Does she go out often?" Francie continued. "Was she out last night?"

"Frenchy!" Jeannette said, "Don't you think you're being a little nosy?"

"Of course she's nosy." Astrid returned from the kitchen carrying some kind of cake. "She's a detective. That's what she gets paid to do."

"I'm getting paid?" Francie asked.

"It's just a figure of speech," Astrid answered.

T.J. had taken the opportunity to slip a meatball under the table to Rusty. Jeannette and Astrid pretended not to notice.

Francie spent the next little while trying to engage T.J. in conversation. She learned not much, as he seemed rather shy. He liked it at the lake. He liked catching frogs. He used to go fishing with his dad but hadn't gone yet this summer. He professed to like to swim, which Francie contested because it seemed to her he was always filthy. "How do you get so dirty?"

He gave a cursory glance at his dusty arms and legs and shrugged.

"Sorry about your friend Warren," Francie said. "That must be hard for you. I understand you were chums."

T.J. looked down. Tears trembled in his eyes.

Francie, still distracted, started scooping cake out of the pan with a spoon. "Why am I dishing this out with a spoon?" she asked.

"I can't find a spatula," Astrid answered. "Just pretend it's pudding."

17
THE FUNERAL

THE FUNERAL was short and nondescript. There was a lunch following, provided by the ladies of Enchantment, the same ladies Warren had helped out so many times in the past. A long table in the church basement was laden with Jell-O salads and hotdishes—casseroles—of all descriptions. Frosted cakes, plates of cookies, and pans of bars weighed down the far end of the table.

Astrid and Jeannette were part of the crew of ladies who had brought the food and were now serving it. Francie had given a halfhearted offer of help, but she was shooed away by women who quickly comprehended that she would only be in the way. So she filled her plate, and since she didn't feel like sitting in the church basement, found her way outside and across the street, where a picnic table offered her fresh air and solitude. Plus maybe a little time to think.

The day had grown so hot she had little appetite. She ate around the mini-marshmallows in the Jell-O and watched people come and go from the church. Heat wavered up from the sidewalk, making the funeral goers appear to undulate slightly. In the thick air, they all seemed a little queasy. Or maybe it was she who was queasy. She eyed her plate with suspicion. She'd purposely avoided the potato salad and wondered what kind of casserole Aunt Astrid had made. She should have thought to find out.

A big taupe SUV peeled into the parking lot, somehow managing to kick up dust, came to a screeching halt, and emptied out Buck, talking on his phone. She strained to hear what he was saying but could catch only some disconnected words. She thought of sneaking closer but stopped when he glanced around, unzipped his fly, and aimed into the hydrangeas.

Francie almost laughed out loud but realized that because he had to talk louder to hear himself, she could now hear what he was saying.

"Yes, I know. No, now listen. There's no need for that—don't—" He paused. "You and I don't see what's the big deal, but believe me, a lot of other people will. It's exactly the kind of thing that gets people all worked up. Yeah, well . . ." he looked at his phone, crammed it in his pocket, and zipped up his pants.

Then he charged into the church while other people began to file out, heading to their cars. Some stopped to chat; some rushed to their cars; others, not realizing they were being observed, did mildly embarrassing things like picking their teeth or noses. Francie smiled to see a small child spit something out of her mouth into her hand, then toss the hateful thing into the bushes. Sandy came out of a side door and rushed away; it must be hard for him to get away from the resort. Mrs. Smattering tottered outside carrying something wrapped in a towel. She spoke for a few moments with Mrs. Hansen. Mrs. Smattering peeled the towel away and opened the lid of a casserole dish and Mrs. Hansen peered inside. They could be two of the three witches in *Macbeth*, Francie thought, chanting, "When shall we meet again? In thunder, lightning, or in rain?" Then the ladies went their separate ways, now looking more like ordinary women off to run their errands.

Ginger exited the church carrying a stack of papers and some books, which she set in the back seat of her car. Then she leaned against the car and lit up a cigarette. Crazy Ginger, Francie thought. She smoked, drank, and taught Sunday school.

When Potter approached from across the lot, Ginger hastily dropped the cigarette and stubbed it out with the heel of her shoe. He really wasn't a bad-looking guy, Francie thought. She wondered how old he was. Ten years older than she was, maybe? Was that too much? Francie told herself to stop thinking like that. He paused to talk to Ginger and—wait a minute! He was stroking her arm! So it was *Potter*! Ginger was going out with Potter! Francie stared in amazement as Potter's hand ran up and down Ginger's arm, petting it as if it were a cat.

She would have liked to ruminate on that for a while, but then the Fredericksons materialized, looking like a mirage of a family as the heat caused that undulating phenomenon.

Mrs. Frederickson minced across the gravel parking lot in her heels. Francie supposed a funeral was not an appropriate time and place to ask for a favor, but no time like the present, right? She stood up and smoothed the same black dress she'd worn to the party (thanks, Ginger), then crossed the street to talk to Mrs. Frederickson.

Mr. Frederickson was a bland-faced man who stood slightly aloof, probably accustomed to people wanting to talk to his wife but not to him. Latice had perfected a look of being bored and irritated at the same time.

"Hi, Mr. Frederickson," Francie said, and he nodded a practiced *I know you don't really want to talk to me* kind of nod. "How are you, Latice?" Francie added, making a quarter-hearted attempt at being friendly.

"Darling!" Mrs. Frederickson chirped, then turned to her husband, "This is the Frye girl. She's a big—"

Francie jumped in. "No!" she cried, then quickly added, "I'm sorry, this isn't exactly how I planned to talk to you about this, but I'm wondering, Mrs. Frederickson, well, you see, I know who you are. That is, I recognized you. You're Frederica Ricard. I love your work! Sorry, I sound like an idiot."

Latice rolled her eyes. Mrs. Frederickson pulled her sunglasses down on her nose and smiled conspiratorially at Francie. "Why, aren't you clever?" she said.

"I—I don't want to be rude, but I'm not really a detective," Francie said in a rush. "People seem to think . . . well, I played a detective on a TV show." ("A children's TV show," she added under her breath.) "Never mind."

"So you aren't really investigating suspicious deaths, then?" Mrs. Frederickson said.

"Oh, well, snooping a little, I guess," Francie said, "but it's not what I do for a living. What I really want to do is act. I'm trying to find some work right now, as a matter of fact."

"Here? In the northwoods?" Mrs. Frederickson laughed.

"No, in New York, but I just wanted to say—" What did she want to say, she wondered. How could she phrase this?

But Mrs. Frederickson was far ahead of her. "Well, that's simply marvelous, darlin'! Isn't it, honey?" She turned to her husband, who smiled wanly, clearly weary of exactly these kinds of encounters. Turning back to Francie, Mrs. Frederickson added brightly, "But my dear, you really *are* a detective, to figure out who I am. Not that I'm trying to keep it a secret or anything, but believe me, nobody around here has a clue about my stage life. It's quite lovely, you know, to travel incognito. So, I'll tell you what: I'll keep your secret if you'll keep mine." She winked at Francie and shoved her sunglasses back up on her nose. "And call me Freddie. All my friends do." She lit a cigarette and went on, "Now, how can I help you? I know! Why, this is perfect! A friend of mine is staying with us for a couple of days. He's a casting agent for a—"

Francie's stomach fluttered. Out of the corner of her eye she saw Latice roll her eyes, shift her weight, and cross her arms.

"Why don't you stop by, let's see, tomorrow evening, about nine? It'll be just us, since hubby and Latice are going to the Twin Cities."

"Wow! Yes! Thanks! Thanks so much! I'll be there."

The Fredericksons climbed into their black Lexus and drove away.

Francie stood in the dusty lot staring after them. As soon as she was fairly sure they couldn't see her in their rearview mirror, she jumped up and down a couple of dozen times until she couldn't jump anymore. A few stragglers stared at her as they left the church and found their cars.

Her aunts and the other ladies were probably starting to clean up by now. Francie knew how to wash dishes; she might as well help. She'd have to wait for her aunts, anyway.

Francie plucked the damp dress away from her body while she walked to the church. Just as she opened the door, a scream pierced the heavy air, and she bolted down the stairs toward the sound. When her eyes adjusted to the dim light, she gasped.

Sprawled on the floor was the pale-skinned, large-bellied, dead-looking body of Buck Thorne. Standing over him, looking as guilty as if she were holding a smoking gun, was Astrid. But it was not a gun she held in her raised hand. It was a spatula.

18

THE COUNTY JAIL

"DON'T SAY ANYTHING!" Francie said, rushing into the sheriff's office.

"Oh, hello, Frenchy," Astrid said. "Rydell, here—"

Francie turned to her aunts and tried to keep her voice steady, "Don't tell him anything. You should have a lawyer present."

"Now, miss," the sheriff said, "nobody's under arrest—yet." He leaned back in his swivel chair. "I'm just askin' a few questions."

"Even so, they should have their lawyer present," Francie said, straining to remember her lines from the show. "You can't hold them if you aren't going to charge them." That wasn't bad, Francie thought. That had been one of her lines.

"I'm sorry, but the evidence points in their direction—especially your aunt Astrid. She was found standing over the dead body of Buck Thorne holding the presumed murder weapon," the sheriff said. "A spatula."

"You're saying the murder weapon was a spatula?" Francie asked.

"Well, no. But the hotdish it was in may have been."

"*What?*"

"There is some evidence that Buck was poisoned."

"Poisoned!" Francie exhaled. "Still, I hardly think that being in possession of a spatula is incriminating. Just because she's holding a spatula doesn't make her a murderer. It could have come from anyone's hotdish!" Francie couldn't believe she had just uttered that sentence, and in all seriousness. Or, in fact, that any of this was actually taking place.

The sheriff consulted a piece of paper. "We've got the ham and pea, the hamburger rice, the tater tot, the chicken wild rice, and that one with the potato chips on it, yet the spatula had tuna noodle on it, which is what was on Buck's plate. The tuna noodle, that's the one we don't got. We sent that spatula in for testing."

"I see. The case of the poisoned spatula," Francie said. Man, why hadn't she had lines like these in her show? "Don't you ever watch crime shows?" she asked. "The person left holding the murder weapon is never the one who actually did it."

"That's on TV, miss," the sheriff said, "and this is real life."

"No, it isn't!" Francie cried. "It can't be! It's too bizarre! Now, listen. Nothing my aunts say can be used against them; you realize that, right? You have to let them call their lawyer."

"I told them they could call their lawyer. They said they'd wait for you."

"We'll *all* wait for their lawyer," Francie said and pulled out her phone. "Auntie, who should I call?" she asked Jeannette.

"Franklin Sage, honey. He's in the book."

"Mr. Sage is not in the office," the voice on the other end said. It sounded as if it belonged to a fourteen-year-old. "It's Wednesday."

"Okay," Francie said. "It's Wednesday, whatever that means. Can you, or better yet, can *I* reach him on his cell phone?"

"I doubt it," the fourteen-year-old said.

"This is pretty serious. One of his clients has been incarcerated."

"Maybe you should take him to the hospital. There's a twenty-four-hour clinic here you can take him to."

"In-car-cer-ated! In jail!"

"Oh!" the young voice came back. "I see. Um, well, I can leave a message for, um, Mr. Sage, and he'll call you in the morning."

"No," Francie said. "Not morning. Now."

"The thing is, he's fishing. But, um, Nels just came in. Should I send him over?"

"Nels?"

"Office intern. He's the only one around today. I think he just got back from fishing, too. Wednesday is fishing day."

"Fine," Francie said. "Whatever." What kind of rinky-dink operation was this? And who was this office intern, Nels? She pictured some skinny, geeky guy, fresh off the debate team. Great, Francie thought glumly. I look forward to meeting him.

While she waited, she checked the messages on her phone. Her grandfather had called, looking for her. He'd left several messages in his deep, authoritative voice, each gaining in intensity: first frustration, then worry, then anger, and finally a threatening "I know where you are and don't think I won't come find you!"

He'd get over it. She hoped.

Nels blew in like a sudden westerly gale, blowsy and fresh, not skinny or geeky. In fact, she recognized him. It was Neptune, although today he looked more like Adonis, wearing a rumpled shirt and dirty shorts and running his hand through his curls that, honestly, had shaped themselves into a completely ridiculous head of hat hair. He seemed too young to work in a law office, Francie thought, but then she was too young to be a detective, wasn't she? Everyone in this town seemed too young for their jobs. Except the sheriff.

Nels wiped his hand on his shorts and offered it to her. His hand was warm and firm and large and comforting and she felt tears spring to her eyes. She fought them back, reminding herself, *I'm the big detective from New York.*

"You must be Francesca," Nels said. "Your aunts have talked about you. And you're—"

"Not a big detective," Francie hurried to finish his sentence. "But don't tell my aunts' friends. They firmly want to believe they know an important detective from New York."

Nels laughed. "Got it," he said. His laugh fit well with the westerly gale impression—also blowsy and fresh.

In the same way he entered—in a whoosh—he had Astrid and Jeannette released simply by speaking a few quiet words to the sheriff.

"You're out on Enchantment, right? Can I give you a lift?"

The idea was so appealing, Francie almost said yes before realizing she had driven and that her aunts' boat waited at the landing.

"My aunt's car is here and their boat is—"

Astrid interrupted. "Oh, if you and Francie could stop and pick up a few things at the store, then Jeannette and I could go straight home and start some dinner for all of us. I'm sure you could borrow a boat from Sandy, so you don't have to launch yours, Nels."

"Auntie, I don't think—" Francie began.

"I could contribute some fresh sunnies," Nels offered.

"Ooh," Astrid squeaked, "won't that be lovely!" She scrawled a few items on a scrap of paper she plucked off the sheriff's desk and handed it to Nels. Pretty weird to send your lawyer to the grocery store for you, but this whole day had been surreal, and when Jeannette said, "Hand over the keys, sweetie," Francie handed them to her without protest.

Then, because Francie must have stood somewhat dazed in the middle of the station, Nels steered her gently toward the door, his warm hand on the small of her back.

19
SUNNIES

"I WONDER WHAT THEY'RE PLANNING to start for dinner," Francie said, peering into the brown paper grocery bags. "It seems we have all the ingredients with us."

When she glanced up, Nels was looking at her. She quickly redirected her gaze back into the bags. But she was left with the distinct impression he was smiling.

"It seems sort of strange to be shopping for olive oil and Shore Lunch, whatever that is," she said, eliciting a raised eyebrow from Nels, "when my aunt is the prime suspect in a murder."

"Tell me how that happened," he said.

While Nels parked his truck in Sandy's lot, Francie filled him in about the scene at the church. She explained how the sheriff had been at the funeral luncheon. He'd made everyone still there stay for questions while he sent samples of the funeral food off to a lab somewhere for testing.

"Why would he suspect foul play?" Nels wondered, whipping off his dirty T-shirt.

"Exactly," Francie said, trying not to gape. "And then some

sort of information arrives that makes him decide to take Astrid in for questioning. 'Question her right here,' I said, but no, the sheriff was going to take her in." Francie tried to keep her mind on the thread of her story while Nels rummaged around in the back of his truck for a different rumpled, but clean, shirt. While he pulled the shirt over his head, she actually heard herself say "buff" instead of "*but* Auntie Jen had gotten herself arrested, or detained, or whatever, too, by assaulting a law officer," which was, in Francie's opinion, a rather extreme interpretation of what had happened. Jeannette had flung herself on the sheriff and wrapped her arms around his neck, which, okay, *did* nearly choke him, but *still*. Francie had peeled Jeannette off and apologized profusely to the sheriff, but to no avail. He'd hauled them in for questioning. "Do you think they're in terrible trouble?" Francie asked Nels.

"No," Nels said. "Rydell is . . . he's all right, really, but—"

"He's all set to retire?"

"Yep," Nels said. "He doesn't want to work too hard. This probably made him feel as if he was doing something. Now he has, and he'll probably let it go."

"Let it go? Poisoning?"

"I'm kind of surprised he even bothered to investigate at all."

"Supposedly Buck is a friend of his."

"Oh, yeah. That's right."

Sandy appeared and said it was okay to borrow a boat for the evening. Her aunts had already asked, he said.

During their dinner of crispy fried sunnies—Francie had forgotten how good they were—and Astrid's unusual potato salad, in which Francie was hard pressed to find a potato, her aunts told their own version of the story. They'd been serving the stragglers at the luncheon and were ready to put everything away when Buck came in. Astrid couldn't remember how that spatula came to be in her hand. But it was her spatula, or anyway, she had one like it, or she used to have one like it. At least she thought she did. At any rate, Jeannette said, she didn't like to say it about anyone, but wasn't it true the world was better off without Buck?

"I'm a little sad about Buck," Francie mused.

"That's very sweet of you," Jeannette said. "I'm ashamed to say that there are those of us who aren't that sad."

"It's not that I'm so sweet, really," Francie said, "but Buck told me he was going to tell me something about my mother."

A look of concern flicked across both her aunts' faces. Nels just looked confused.

"What kind of thing?" Astrid said.

"I don't know!" Francie cried. "And now I'll never know."

"I can't imagine he could have known anything about her," Jeannette said. "He probably said that to keep you from talking."

"Maybe," Francie mumbled.

"Well, now that he's gone, we won't have to worry anymore," Astrid added and smacked her lips.

"You might have to worry about being arrested for murder!" Francie said.

"Oh *that*," Jeannette said. "That's just ridiculous, isn't it, Astrid?"

Astrid didn't answer.

"Astrid!" Jeannette said. "Didn't you hear me? I said it's ridiculous for you to be arrested for murder. Rydell will come to his senses and see it couldn't be you."

Nels had been amazingly silent throughout the conversation, Francie thought. But he did seem to be busy picking bones out of his fish.

"What kind of hotdish did you make for the funeral, Astrid?" Francie asked, holding her breath for the answer.

"Why, I made salmagundi, of course!" she answered, and all four of them breathed again. "With tuna!" she finished.

"Well, did you poison it?" Francie asked.

Nels snorted. So he *was* paying attention.

"Of course not!" Astrid said.

"Where did it go?"

"The poison?"

"The hotdish," Francie said.

"Gone," Astrid said.

"You mean all eaten up?" Francie asked.

"No," Astrid answered. "I mean gone as in *poof!* I don't know!"

"What did the dish look like?" Nels asked.

"The casserole dish?" Astrid said. "It was that brown pottery one, with fish swimming around the sides of it, with a lid, of course."

Francie thought of Mrs. Smattering and Mrs. Hansen clucking over a casserole in the parking lot of the church. Had it been a brown pottery dish? Francie wished she'd paid closer attention. Her TV detective character would have noticed something like that. Why wasn't Francie more like her?

Later, Francie walked Nels out onto the dock.

"Isn't it kind of dark to drive a boat?" she said.

"It's got lights." He jumped in and switched on the lights. "See?" he said. "Red on the port side, green on the starboard side." He reached for the ignition.

"Um," she said. "Um," she said again. *Idiot!* "Do you . . . would you like to talk? I mean, I could really use some help."

"Help?"

"There's so much weirdness around here. All these people dying."

"What?" He looked up at her.

"Listen. Do you want some watermelon?" *That was stupid!*

"Watermelon? Sure." Nels climbed out of the boat while she retrieved a watermelon from the spring where it had been chilling. It was so cold she could barely hold it. She grabbed a big knife from the boathouse and said, "Come on. We can go sit on the roof."

They climbed the path that wound around to the flat roof of the little house. A railing of dubious safety ran around the perimeter of the deck, which was furnished with some rickety chairs and a table that wobbled as she sliced open the watermelon. She handed a big chunk to Nels and took one for herself, and they leaned—carefully—on the railing, spitting seeds down into the lake.

"Didn't I see you at that party at the Fredericksons'?" Francie asked.

He nodded.

"Why?"

"Why what?" he said.

"Why were you there?" she asked.

'Why were *you* there?'

"I asked you first."

"Well," he said, "there's this girl . . ."

Right, Francie thought. It figured. It was always this way; there was always a girl. "Oh," she said. "Latice?"

"No," he said. "I don't think you met her." He cleared his throat. "She—"

"Never mind." Francie cut him off. "It's none of my business." She felt the usual disappointment and then a little wavelet of relief. Her heart would remain unthreatened inside its silver box.

The evening was still. They sat on the rickety chairs for a while listening to the small sounds along the lakeshore. It was so quiet you could hear the clatter of dishes and the tinking of silverware being washed after dinner, the soft closing of screen doors, even voices from far down the way.

Francie spoke quietly as she began to tell Nels about the strange deaths along the shore, about Buck's confession, if that's what it had been, about her aunts' suspicions, about Warren's death, supposedly a suicide, and now this: Buck, poisoned.

"Tell me what happened at the funeral," Nels said.

"Buck arrived late," Francie said. "I saw him drive up and take a piss in the parking lot while talking on his cell phone." (Nels laughed at this.) "I thought he was probably going to pretend that he'd been at the funeral, but he was pretty late. He had to eat after everyone else had finished. It was a hot day. Could he have just eaten a hotdish that had gone bad in the heat? But even then he couldn't die that fast, or at all, could he? The sheriff thinks that one of the hotdishes was poisoned. But where did the hotdish go? And why wasn't *everyone* poisoned? Do you think it's possible the ladies were—?" She stopped herself. "A number of them have a motive," she murmured.

"What?" Nels said.

"It could be almost anybody along this side of the lake. Mrs. Smattering, whose son was killed by the tree branch. Mrs. Hansen, whose husband drowned. And what about Mrs. Simonsen, whose husband died of snakebite? She doesn't live here anymore, but that doesn't mean she might not murder someone. Or, heck, maybe it was *all* of them."

"What are you talking about?"

Francie explained that maybe the elderly ladies had come up with a devious plan to knock Buck off. She *had* seen two of them chattering and clucking over a casserole dish together.

Nels stroked his chin in mock seriousness and said, "Iocane powder. They've been eating it for years to build up an immunity, like the Dread Pirate Roberts, so they could partake in the poisoned hotdish."

"Yes," Francie said. It was a little uncanny how she and Nels seemed to think alike. She'd been thinking of that exact thing from one of her favorite movies, *The Princess Bride*. He *would* like the same movies she did.

"Okay, but seriously," she said. "How was it that only Buck keeled over dead after the funeral lunch? I mean, if there was a poisoned hotdish, wouldn't there be a lot of dead people now?"

"You'd have to think so," Nels agreed.

Francie squeezed her eyes shut and tried to remember what and who she'd seen. Sandy had left in a hurry. Potter had been in a rush, but he had paused to stroke Ginger's arm. Ginger had seemed nervous, but she often did. Then Francie had gotten so distracted with the Fredericksons she probably missed seeing the murderer, missed all the clues. She really was a lousy detective.

"You're mulling pretty hard over there," Nels said.

She laughed ruefully. "There was one point when I thought I had it all figured out and thought maybe I *should* be a detective—that I was so good at it!"

"You're doing all right," Nels said, laying a hand on her arm, which caused a little electricity to pulse through her.

"Did you say Buck took a call on his cell?" he asked.

"Yeah."

"What did he say?"

"Not much." She thought back. "Let's see. He said something like, 'You and I don't see what the big deal is, but believe me, this is exactly the kind of thing people get all worked up about."

"What was he talking about?"

"Beats me."

"It should be easy enough to find out who called him. I'll see what I can do tomorrow."

"Do you think the sheriff will arrest Astrid?" she asked.

"Pretty skimpy evidence—poison on a spatula. Could have been anyone's spatula. Anyone could have tampered with a hotdish or, for that matter, the food on a spatula."

Francie leaped up. "Come on!" she said, grabbing Nels's hands and pulling him out of his chair.

"What? Where are we going?"

Francie pulled a flashlight out of her jacket pocket and flicked it on. "Let's see if we can find this hotdish. The last place it was seen was the church. Let's start there and see if we can either find it or find a clue or something."

"Even if we find it, I'm not sure it'll be worth much as evidence anymore. Anyway, won't the church be locked at this hour?" he asked.

"Yeah, you're probably right." Francie chewed her lip. "I know! Ginger. She teaches Sunday school. Maybe she has a key. Let's go find her."

20
T.J.

"Uh . . . KEY?" Ginger said.

"To the church," Francie repeated.

"Uh . . ." Ginger said.

"Ginger!" Francie snapped. "Are you drunk?"

"No." She slumped into a chair. "It's T.J."

"What?" Francie asked. "What's happened?"

"I don't know," Ginger said. "He's gone. He hasn't come home."

"Oh, God."

"I've been out looking. I just came in now to get a different flashlight. The batteries are going on this one."

"When is the last time you saw him?"

"He was home for dinner, and I thought he went to bed."

"Did he?"

"You can see for yourself." Ginger led them to a modest room at the back of the cabin. The single bed had been tidily made, just one corner of the covers turned back with a small (and dirty) indent on the pillow. Next to the bed stood a small side table on which teetered a baseball-themed lamp and a tall stack of old *National Geographics*. T.J.'s clothes hung neatly in the closet.

"Tidy kid," Nels remarked.

"Yes, he's kind of organized," Ginger said.

"Isn't it odd that he's such a dirtball?" Francie mused.

"How is this helping us?" Ginger wailed. "We should be looking for him."

"You're right," Francie said, "but I'm just trying to think where he might be." Her eyes landed on a door, which she crossed to and opened. "There's a door to the outside in his room," she noted.

"Yeah," Ginger said. "I suppose he just pretended to go to bed and then got up and left. But why?"

"Ginger," Francie said. "He could go out often without you noticing, couldn't he?"

"Yes."

"And he does, doesn't he?"

"Yes," Ginger mumbled.

"You were out looking for him the other day when I came by this way from that party at the Fredericksons'." Francie stole a quick glance at Nels who was thumbing through the stack of magazines.

"Yes." Ginger sank onto the bed and buried her face in the pillow. "But this is the latest he's ever stayed out."

"What time is it?" Francie asked Nels.

He looked at his phone. "After one. Where does he go?"

Ginger shook her head and sobbed into the pillow. "I don't know! I don't press him. I just figured he needed time to sort everything out. Plus, he wasn't bugging me, so I didn't really care what he did. Oh, I'm a terrible sister!"

"You're doing fine, Ginger," Francie comforted her. "Hey, I ran around like a wild banshee when I was a kid. It was glorious to have so much freedom. Every kid should have a place like this."

"Yeah, but when we were kids it was safe. People weren't getting killed left and right."

"So you don't think these deaths have been accidental, either?" Nels asked.

"Yes. No. I don't know!" Ginger wailed. "What's happened to him? Oh, it's all my fault."

"Should we call the police?" Nels asked.

Ginger bit her lip. "Not yet."

Francie tried to convey in a glance to Nels that the whole police thing was complicated for Ginger. Francie could only imagine how hard it would be, given that the sheriff was convinced Ginger's mom had killed her husband.

"All they can do is look—just like us," Ginger added.

"They might not do anything until daylight, anyway," Nels said. He spun the flashlight in his hand like a gunslinger with a six-shooter. "Let's go, partner," he said.

How had it gotten so dark? Francie wondered. Their flashlight beams cast yellow splotches on tree trunks, brush, leaves, branches. It was hard to tell what things were.

"Maybe we should split up," Francie said. "We can cover more ground. Ginger, go down by the lake, along the shore. Nels, you can follow along the path again, and I'll take a trail back into the woods."

"Stay within earshot," Nels said.

When Francie was a kid, there'd been paths leading behind the cabins into the woods: trails to blueberry patches and beaver dams and deer stands and tree forts. If there were any trails now, they were very hard to find in the dark with just a flashlight. She crashed around in the woods for a bit and somehow stumbled onto something, maybe just a deer trail, but enough of a path to follow. She kept expecting it to end at a compost heap or a brush pile, but the path just kept going and going and she became so absorbed that she forgot to call out or to listen for Nels's shouts. All she heard was the wind in the trees: a *whoosh*, fading into silence, then another *whoosh*.

But overlaid on this was a different sound. Not soft. Harsh. Metallic. That same strange sound she had heard the first night. A rhythmic *ka-chink*. It seemed like a familiar noise that she should be able to identify, but she couldn't place it. She moved toward the sound, stopped, listened, moved again. It grew louder; she drew closer, creeping so cautiously she was almost tiptoeing. If she'd been watching herself in a movie, she knew she'd have been yelling, "Turn around, you idiot!" but she couldn't keep herself from moving toward the sound. As she got near to the source, she turned her flashlight off and crept very quietly up the rise of a hill.

Below her was a clearing, awash in moonlight, but in the middle of the open space there was a pool of much brighter light. It took Francie a moment to realize the light came from a headlamp worn by a person working with a shovel. Of course! she thought, a shovel! Now the sound made sense. But what was this person doing? Burying something? Or digging something up? Was he carving out chunks of peat to sell to Home Depot, like Jeannette suggested? Or was it something more sinister?

Francie sneaked closer, keeping her eyes on the now kneeling figure. She hardly dared to breathe, because it certainly felt like whatever was happening here was a secret. There was little other explanation for middle-of-the-night shoveling.

A shout behind her caused her to jump. It was Nels, yelling her name. At the sound, the shoveler looked up, and the headlamp beam swung in her direction and swept over her before she dove into the woods.

She ran, or tried to, crashing through brush, clambering over fallen trees, pushing aside branches. Was the shoveler following her?

Glancing over her shoulder, she could see a bobbling light, and then nothing. It was as if the forest had closed in, almost protectively, behind her. She stopped for a moment and stared into the dark woods. How was it that the woods that had so frightened her before now seemed to be actually helping her?

Turning, she saw the faint, bobbing light of Nels's flashlight far down the path. She raced toward it.

"We found him!" he called. "We've got T.J.!"

By the time they got back to Ginger's, T.J. was tucked into bed, with Ginger standing guard by the door.

"Where was he?" Francie asked.

"Don't know," Ginger said. "When I asked him, he just shrugged. Maybe he'll talk tomorrow. No more questions now. It's two thirty, and he needs to sleep."

Francie and Nels walked away from Ginger's in silence. Once out of earshot, Francie said, "Nels, somebody's back there. With a shovel. Either burying something or digging something up, I don't know, but whoever it was saw me, I'm pretty sure."

"You think he got a good look at you?" Nels asked.

"Yeah," she said. "That, and you called out my name."

"Sorry," Nels said. "Should we go see if we can find whoever it is?"

"Really? Are you serious? You want to?" Francie asked.

"Come on." Nels took her hand in his own. She could let that big, warm hand lead her anywhere.

They retraced their steps to Ginger's cabin, then crunched

into the woods. Francie looked for the path she'd found the first time, but even with two flashlights, she couldn't seem to find it again.

"There was a path," she said, crashing through the brush. "Maybe over here?" More crashing around. "Maybe the other direction." Francie was so turned around, she didn't know what direction they were going. "I think he's gone," she said. "I don't hear that shoveling noise anymore."

"You're probably right," Nels agreed.

They crashed out of the brush into a blessedly open grove of pines and finally back into Ginger's yard. "I'm sorry about all this," Francie said.

"Don't apologize. Seriously. This has definitely been the most unusual evening, or night, or," he yawned, "early morning I've spent in a long time. The yawn means nothing. Really."

Francie walked Nels onto the dock and helped untie the boat. The first hint of sunrise spread across the lake like a pink satin sheet, with small, pale clouds tossed on the water like throw pillows.

"Are you sure you have to go?" she asked. "You could catch some sleep here if you want. I could sleep in the cabin and you can have the boathouse."

"I gotta be at work pretty early," Nels said, climbing aboard. "I better go. You got a lock on that door?" he asked, nodding at the boathouse.

"Yeah," she answered.

"Use it," he said.

21
GONE TO JAIL

FRANCIE WOKE WITH A PLAN. She would take a swim, cool her scratches from the previous night, scrub with Fels-Naptha soap to remove any poison ivy oil, apply aloe to her bites, and brood. She planned to brood on the following issues: Who might have killed Buck Thorne? Whom had she seen back in the peat bog last night? What had he or she been doing? Where had T.J. been? What was she going to do about her grandfather? And where had Aunt Astrid's hotdish gone?

But before she started thinking about anything, she needed a cup of coffee.

She climbed the stairs to the cabin and opened the screen door. "Aunt Astrid?" she said. "Jeannette?"

No answer. But she'd known they wouldn't answer as soon as she stepped in; she'd sensed the emptiness of the place.

Then she saw the note: "Gone to Jail. Coffee cake in kitchen. Help yourself."

Oh, for the love of Mike! She had slept through the whole

thing: the sheriff coming, arresting them, taking them away in a boat. How had she not heard the boat motor? Ridiculous!

Francie grabbed the car keys from off the kitchen table, crammed a piece of coffee cake into her mouth, and ran down the stairs to the boathouse. There she stuffed her wallet into her bag and dashed down the dock to the boat.

The motor roared to life, and Francie drove the boat across the lake, docked it at Sandy's, hurried past the surprised Sandy to her aunts' car, and finally on the drive to town had time to review what she had meant to be thinking about, which had taken on a special urgency. She would have to find the killer if she wanted to get her aunts out of jail, because for sure Rydell wasn't going to do much about it, especially since he thought he had caught the killers already.

Who might have wanted to kill Buck? Considering his personality, probably lots of people. She recollected that his ex-wife, Rose, had thrown a glass of wine on him at the party. Who would know what Rose might have been mad about? Who else might have ill will toward Buck? Buck Jr., maybe? Maybe that receptionist at Paradise Realty knew something. She probably knew everything. Francie would go see her today.

Francie moved on to the next item on her mental checklist. What had she seen last night, exactly? Who might have been back in the peat bog, and what had that person been doing? She had heard Buck Jr. say he had found treasure. "In there," he had said. He must have meant *in the woods*. He had found something in the woods, was digging it up, and Francie had stumbled on it.

She'd have to follow up on that.

Francie charged into the sheriff's office, clipping an elderly gentleman and causing him to drop a package he was carrying. Francie stooped to pick it up.

"Francesca!" the man said sharply.

"Granddad!" Francie choked out when she looked up. "What a surprise."

"I'll bet it is, young lady. Can you please explain what kind of trouble you're in?"

"Oh, *she's* not in any trouble," the sheriff said, sauntering up to them belly first. "It's her aunts who are in trouble."

Francie watched one bushy white eyebrow rise in that slow, ominous way it did when her grandfather was about to disapprove of something.

"I'd like to say that I am surprised, but I can't say that I am," he said.

"Granddad . . ." Francie pleaded.

"I'm pleased that you're not in trouble, but I am displeased about many other things. Shall I list them?" Without waiting for her answer, he continued, "One, not consulting me about your plans to travel. Two, traveling on your own without permission. Three, not returning my phone calls. Four, lying about your whereabouts."

"I didn't lie!" Francie protested, then remembered Buck's explanation about sins of commission and omission. Maybe she had lied by omission. "Okay, maybe I did kind of lie, but that's because I knew you wouldn't approve, and—"

"You're darn tootin' I don't approve. Not one little bit. Here you are, back in the bosom of your aunts who are reliable in only one thing, and that is their nuttiness. Now they are in jail no doubt for some cockamamie scheme they cooked up."

"Actually, they're in for murder," the sheriff offered.

Francie would have liked to punch the amused look off his face. "Excuse me?" she said to the sheriff. "What happened to 'presumed innocent'?"

"Those are the charges," the sheriff said. "That's all I meant. Jeannette is named as an accessory."

Her grandfather dabbed at his forehead with a handkerchief. "I've got two tickets home," he said. "Flight leaves tomorrow, so I'll give you the rest of today to get your things together and say good-bye to your aunts. Meet me in the lobby of the Inn on the Lake at ten o'clock tomorrow morning."

"I can't go now," Francie said. "I'm not going to go when Aunt Astrid and Aunt Jeannette are in jail. I've got to prove they didn't do it."

"Pfft!" Her grandfather waved his hand dismissively. "Young lady, you're not even old enough to be considered a young lady. You're just a girl. Leave this sort of thing to the professionals. Law enforcement will take care of it."

"No, they won't!" Francie fought the urge to bring her foot down in a petulant little stamp. She refused to look at the sheriff, because she knew he was smirking.

"Tomorrow we leave for the city," her grandfather said.

"Why are you being so unreasonable?" Francie asked. "Anyway, I'm not going."

"I don't think I need to remind you of certain financial realities," her grandfather said.

Francie groaned inwardly. The trust fund, which he held over her head at every opportunity.

"If you continue to demonstrate this kind of immaturity, I may have to move the age at which you can access your fund."

"Come *on!*" Francie cried. "You can't seriously think I'm going to leave my aunts in this predicament."

"They got themselves into it; they can get themselves out of it," her grandfather said.

"You know what, Granddad?" Francie said. "You're heartless. You could be using your influence to help, you know, instead of making things *worse*. You don't have to be such a curmudgeon."

"That's quite enough, Francesca," her grandfather said, and spun around, then turned back and handed her the package he was carrying. "You know where the post office is, I assume. Please mail this for me." He handed her some cash, which she stuffed in her pocket, then he finished by saying, "I'll see you in the morning." He pushed the door open and disappeared down the street.

As if she had nothing else to do but mail packages all day!

Francie took a moment to collect herself before turning to face Sheriff Johnson.

"You must have been out partying last night," he said from his swivel chair, looking her up and down.

Francie glowered at him. "You haven't the slightest idea what I was doing last night or what I saw. While you're busy arresting helpless old ladies—"

"I don't know about helpless." The sheriff pointed to his black eye.

Francie winced.

"So," the sheriff continued, "your grandfather don't seem impressed by your—"

"Just tell me what's going on," Francie cut him off.

Sheriff Johnson waved a piece of paper at her. "We got the report back from the lab." Francie glanced at the black dog sprawled alongside his desk. "Not that one," he said. "The lab in Minneapolis. There were traces of cyanide found on the spatula."

"Cyanide?" Francie squawked. "That should convince everyone it *wasn't* Astrid. Everybody would believe it if she poisoned him with ptomaine or salmonella or something. Everyone's afraid of Astrid's casseroles exactly because of that. But cyanide? Where would she even get such a thing? And anyway she may or may not have dished out poisoned food, but that doesn't mean she's the one who put the poison in it."

"We got the fingerprints. We got the evidence. We got the results."

"A motive?" Francie asked. "Do you have that? Why would Astrid want to kill Buck?"

"Now, don't be too worried," the sheriff said, leaning in toward her and lowering his voice. "I'm sure they'll get off with some kind of insanity plea."

"They're not insane!" Francie cried.

"Now, don't be too hasty," the sheriff said. "I'll pretend I didn't hear you. Like I said: we got the fingerprints, the evidence, the results." The sheriff waved the sheet of paper again. "What we don't got is the hotdish. Maybe you should see if you can find that."

"Maybe I should see if I can find them their lawyer," she said, and made a point of using the sheriff's phone to make the call.

Mr. Sage was in a meeting, the receptionist said, but he would speak with her aunts this afternoon. Yes, of course, he would give her a call.

Francie was trembling when she stepped out of the sheriff's office. She had one day—one day!—to get her aunts out of jail. That meant one day to figure everything out: Who was the killer, or killers? Who was the mysterious shoveler? Where was T.J. going at night?

Maybe she didn't have to figure *everything* out, but there was still a murderer on the loose, somewhere. Though the day was warm and getting warmer, a chill traveled down her spine.

Or she could defy her grandfather . . . Oh, boy, she shouldn't even be thinking this way. He held the purse strings in the form of the trust fund she had been counting on to give her the freedom she so desired. Was it worth yet more years of being under Granddad's thumb to defy him this one time? If he said he'd bump up the age at which she could access the money, he meant it.

That meant she had to solve everything today. Now.

No problem!

First, she would follow up her hunch to check on potential enemies of Buck Thorne. That meant a visit to Paradise Realty.

Darcee the receptionist was not-so-surreptitiously texting under the desk.

Francie startled her when she said her name.

"Oh!" Darcee said. "Didn't hear you come in."

"Do you mind if I ask you a few questions?" Francie asked.

"Fire away," Darcee said, glancing at her phone.

"Just wondering if you know anybody who might want to see Buck Sr. dead."

"Are you a P.I. or something?"

"No," Francie said simply. She was planning to *ask* the questions, not answer them.

"Well, pretty much everybody had a reason to, I suppose," Darcee said. "He's like the perfect murder victim 'cuz everybody hated him. Like those murder mysteries when everybody hates the guy who gets killed, so everybody is a suspect."

"You, too?"

"Well, he was kind of obnoxious," Darcee said. "But wait! I didn't hate him that much! I didn't kill him! I mean, I could be out of a job now, you know?"

"I'm not accusing you," Francie said. "What about his ex-wife, Rose?"

"Yeah, she hated him, too. But why would she kill him? Then the alimony payments would stop, right?" Darcee said.

"How about Buck Jr.?" Francie asked.

The receptionist's face became a mask of thinly disguised disgust. "What about him?"

"Did he get along with his dad?"

"His stepdad, you mean?"

"Oh?" Francie said. Maybe the idea of Buck Jr. as the killer was less remote than she thought. "Well, did they get along, the two of them?"

"They fought some," Darcee said. "Mostly over money. Buck Jr. always wanted money."

"What did he want it for?"

"What *didn't* he want it for?" Darcee said. "Usually money for one of his toys. Like that big speedboat."

"That great big boat is Buck Jr.'s?"

"Yeah, I think so," Darcee said. "He was always needing gas money for it. Or for his diving obsession."

"Diving? Scuba diving?"

Darcee nodded. "He's really into it."

"He does it around here?"

"I guess. Don't know what he finds. There's not really anything very pretty to look at, like in the Bahamas or something. Just brown fish, brown rocks, brown sand, brown weeds. Ick."

"Has he ever said anything to you about finding something?" Francie asked, steering the conversation back to the issue.

"Like what?"

"Some kind of treasure, maybe?"

Darcee snorted. "Well, he does like to brag about stuff, but then you never know if he's just making it up or what. Like he told me he finally found that treasure out at Enchantment. Ha!"

Francie caught her breath. "Did he say anything else about it? Anything more specific about where?"

Darcee looked up at her and gave her a pitying glance before turning her attention back to her phone. "I wouldn't get jazzed about it. Buck is so full of bull."

"Humor me," Francie said. "It's not like I'm going to go dig it up myself or anything."

"Oh, he's not digging anything up," Darcee said. "He says the treasure is under Enchantment."

"Under enchantment? Like bewitched?" Francie asked.

"No," Darcee answered. "Under *Enchantment*. Under the *lake*."

22
DQ

WITH HER HEAD SPINNING, Francie stepped out onto the street. She was getting nowhere, and she only had this one day to figure everything out. I've already thought about that enough, she scolded herself. Still, she couldn't help wondering if there was any way she could defy her grandfather and stay. She really didn't want to estrange him. He was exasperating, but she did love him, and she knew he loved her, too. It was just that he had all these rules. She had to do this or that or the other thing unless this, that, or the other thing. She was under his thumb unless she could get a paid job, a real paid—wait a minute! There was one hope. A glimmer of hope. The audition with the casting agent. Tonight! She knew it wasn't really an audition, but it sort of was. If she could get a real acting job, a paying job, she wouldn't have to rely on her grandfather for money, and she'd be free to come and go as she pleased. She'd need to make a good impression at the Fredericksons' tonight. She'd need something decent to wear. For cry-eye! she thought, am I really wondering about what I'm going to wear at a time like this?

Apparently yes, she realized, as she pushed open the door to the one plausible clothing store in town. Well, she needed time to think. She might as well think while scraping hangers along a rack. She wondered if she should have prepared a short monologue or a song . . . She was never going to find anything she wanted to wear in this store, was she? While longing for her favorite East Village thrift store, she wondered if there was a piano at the Fredericksons'. Otherwise, she could do that speech from—she stopped in midthought. There it was—in the midst of loon appliqués and sailboat-themed clothes—a little black knit shift shot through with gold thread that made the dress glint as if it were fresh in from the rain. In this dress she could do everything from Shakespeare to musical comedy. She could probably sing opera in this dress—if she could sing opera.

She gulped at the price. She couldn't afford that! Then she remembered the cash her grandfather had given her and pulled it out of her pocket. A hundred bucks! The money was plunked down on the counter; the dress bought. Granddad was already mad at her—how much worse could it get?

At the post office, she ran into Potter, his arms full of packages.

"That must be tricky," she said.

"Tricky?" he said.

"I mean, to pack your pots so they don't break." Then she thought of his lumpy, heavy pots and realized you'd practically have to take a sledgehammer to them to break them.

He mumbled something about knowing how to pack the pots, then turned and walked out, leaving a little trail of dry clay from his dirty shoes. She had to brush off the crumbled clay he'd left on the counter before setting down her grandfather's package.

After that errand was completed, she wondered whether to go to the law office to see if Mr. Sage was available. That would be *one* reason to go there.

Her phone buzzed. It was Sage.

"We'll get it all straightened out," he said. His voice was deep and reassuring. She pictured a rotund, Santa Claus–like figure. "Don't worry. I'll call you this afternoon."

So Francie had no reason, well, no *legitimate* reason, to go to the law office, and she walked by the door once, then twice, before turning and stepping inside. A receptionist sat behind a desk just inside the door, and she asked if she might speak to Nels, adding, "If he's busy, it's no problem. I shouldn't bother him at work. You know what? Just tell him never mind."

"Just tell *who* never mind?"

Francie turned to see Nels leaning against the door to an office, looking clean and pressed in a nice, crisp shirt and tie. How did he *do* that? The sleeves of his shirt were rolled up; the scratches on his arms made him look manly and tough, like he'd been wrestling bobcats. Her scratches made her look insane, like she wore barbed wire bracelets or something.

He seemed happy to see her, which came as a pleasant surprise.

"Come on," he said. "You want a DQ?"

"DQ?"

"Dairy Queen."

She squinted at him.

"You don't have Dairy Queens in New York?"

"We have Queens in New York," she said. "Also queens."

Nels laughed. "Who'd think New York would be so very far behind on providing its populace with mono- and diglycerides?"

"What did you say this stuff was made of again?" she asked, hurrying to lick up the drips as the cone melted into a puddle.

"Never mind," Nels said. "You look terrible, by the way."

"Thank you," Francie said. "And you're so charming."

"That's me." Nels led her across the street to a park where they sat on the playground swings. "Is it true your great-aunts are in jail?" he asked.

"Things are worse than you can imagine." Francie almost cried into her ice cream. She explained about her aunts and about how her grandfather upbraided her as if she were a child in front of the sheriff, ruining her credibility. And now her granddad wanted her to leave with him first thing in the morning. She didn't know what she was going to do.

"So not much time," Nels said. "Have you come up with any new leads?"

"Well, I tried to think who would be back in the woods, and I remembered hearing Buck Jr. tell his dad that he had found the treasure at Enchantment. There's a legend about a treasure."

Nels reached over and wiped a spot of ice cream off her nose. "Okay, I don't want to shoot anything down, but has anybody suggested to you that Buck Jr. is—"

"Full of BS?"

"Yeah."

"Yeah," Francie said. "Darcee, at the office. Okay, so you say it, too. Maybe he's a whack job. Here's another thing: I saw Potter at the post office. His clothes were dirty, like he might have been shoveling dirt. Maybe it was Potter."

"Who's Potter?"

"He's a potter."

"And you suspect him because his clothes were dirty?"

"I mean, really dirty—like T.J.'s."

"Frenchy!" Nels said. "He's a potter. He works with clay. What would you expect?"

"Yeah, I guess you're right. Okay, I'm reaching." She made circles in her swing, twisting the chains around and around, then letting go until the swing spun loose. "I just want this all to make sense. I *need* it to! I thought I had it all figured out, and then it fell apart when Buck was poisoned. Now nothing makes sense anymore. There are so many unanswered questions."

"Like . . . ?"

"One: Warren. Did he or did he not commit suicide? My aunts are pretty convinced it wasn't suicide. If that's true, who killed him? Buck? Then who killed Buck? Was it the same killer both times? And what about all the other "accidental" deaths? Buck basically confessed to some of them, but not all. Was someone else also arranging accidental deaths? Why?"

"That's question number *one*? What's question number *two*?"

"T.J. disappearing for long sojourns. Related?"

"Could be nothing but kid stuff."

"Do you think he's been back there digging, too?" she said. "That would explain the dirty clothes. The first day I was here, Ginger teased him about digging, um, something silly. Elephant bones."

"I used to dig up elephant bones when I was a kid," Nels said, devouring the last of his cone.

Francie looked at him. "Around here?"

"Yeah. More or less."

"Find a lot?"

"I think they were mostly moose bones," Nels admitted.

"So do you think T.J. is digging up moose bones?"

"Kid who reads *National Geographics*?" Nels said. Francie remembered the stack of them next to T.J.'s bed. Nels was observant, she thought. "He might actually know an elephant bone when he sees one."

"But, come on. Seriously. Elephant bones?" Francie said.

"Sure. The biggest elephants that ever lived: mammoths. During the Pleistocene era, there were mammoths running all over the place around here. Or lumbering or whatever they did. Mastodons, too. They're the two main elephant types during the Ice Age. It's conceivable they could be found around here."

Francie stared at Nels. What was he doing with one of those sparkly-haired, friends-of-Latice who populated the Fredericksons' party? Guys! A smart girl wouldn't fall for a dim guy, but the reverse was not always the case.

"So you think he's digging up mammoth bones?"

"I'm just saying," he said. That adorable smile played on his lips. Francie couldn't stop staring at his lips. Fortunately, he started swinging, pumping his legs to make himself soar into the air, his tie flying behind him. "Come on," he said. "Keep up!"

"But why in the dark? In the middle of the night?" Francie wondered aloud. She pulled herself and her swing back as far as she could, then flew.

"Impossible to say," Nels said. "You need to talk to T.J."

"Yeah," Francie said. "I'll go talk to him this afternoon. But, anyway, about Buck Jr.: don't you think that's worth following up on at least?"

"Buck is usually not that hard to locate. Just find his boat."

"Ah, yes, the boat."

"If you want, I'll come with you. But I gotta work until five."

"Naw," Francie jumped off the swing. "I'm just going to go see if I can find him."

"Don't do anything foolish," Nels said. "Frenchy?"

She turned back.

"Did you hear me?"

"Uh-huh," she said, but she already knew she would do whatever it took to find out what was going on.

23

A SECRET

Buck's boat was not at the dock.

"Sandy!" she said, barging into the store. "Is Buck out on the lake?"

Sandy looked up from the cash register, his face flushed with a curious mix of surprise and anger. "Buck Jr.?" he growled. "Yeah, he's out there. Why?"

"What's the matter?" she asked.

"Just a minute," he said.

While she waited until he finished with his customer, Francie looked around the store at the old maps, pictures, posters, an arrowhead collection in a glass case, and an ancient illuminated Hamm's Beer sign with a picture of a red canoe on a shimmering, somewhat mesmerizing lake.

"Mesmerizing, isn't it?" Sandy said, his voice in her ear.

Francie jumped. "I don't remember that arrowhead collection," she said. "Has that always been there?"

"Seems like it's always been there," Sandy said.

"Are you mad at Buck about something?" she asked, as they walked to the shore.

"He's up to something." Sandy put a pair of binoculars to his eyes. "See that island? I'll bet anything Buck is on the other side of it. I'd like to know for sure what he's doing out there."

"Wait. What? He's on that island?"

"No, in his boat on the other side of it. I don't like it, and I don't trust him."

This didn't make sense. The island was miles from where she'd been last night when she'd heard the shoveling. "Can we go check it out?"

Sandy shook his head. "I can't. I'm the only one here right now."

"I guess I can go look for him in the boat," Francie suggested.

"No," Sandy said. "Take a kayak. You can sneak up that way: quiet, small, low in the water, not very noticeable. If you take your boat, he'll see you coming. Keep yourself behind the island, so he can't see you, then pull your kayak up on this side and walk over to the other side. You might be able to see what he's up to. Do it so he can't see you, though, or he'll quit. He's being supersecretive. Here, take these." He handed her the binoculars.

A customer called to Sandy from the store.

"Help yourself," Sandy told Francie, gesturing to the kayaks, paddles, and life jackets. "You know how to paddle a kayak, right?"

"Uh . . . huh," Francie answered, but Sandy was already gone. Well, how hard could it be? She'd seen pictures of people kayaking. She looked again at the island. How long would this take? Maybe ten minutes to paddle out there, five minutes to see what he was doing, ten minutes back. Half an hour, total. She could afford that. It might be worth it.

She tucked her purse and the shopping bag with the cute

dress wrapped up in scented tissue paper into the storage compartment and shoved the little yellow kayak out into the water. How were you supposed to get in? she wondered. Keep your center of gravity low, she surmised. Butt first.

She slid gracelessly into the boat and was immediately struck by how tippy it seemed—like it might flip over any minute, and then what would happen? Would she be stuck in it, upside down?

She didn't think about this for long, because the paddle was in her hand and the island was in her sight, and as she paddled, she got used to the tippy feeling. And she became captivated by her loon's-eye view of the world. It was not so much being *on* the water as being *in* it, almost like being part of the water—the way a duck or a loon is, half the body submerged.

A light breeze kicked up small, friendly waves that sparkled so fiercely she could imagine herself paddling in an enormous vat of diamonds. It was so quiet. The waves tapped softly against her craft; somewhere in the distance gulls squabbled like fussy toddlers; a boat motor droned far, far away as if in her imagination, yet she felt surrounded by silence. It almost made her anxiety dissolve. Almost.

At the island, Francie beached the boat, got out awkwardly, and pulled the boat up onto the shore. She suspected it had taken longer than she'd thought to paddle to the island; she'd have to keep this surveillance mission short.

She hurried as much as she dared while still trying to be stealthy, creeping over the rise of the island and down the other side, finally ensconcing herself behind a tree. She didn't really need binoculars; she could see well enough an orange flag attached to a buoy—it looked like a diving flag. Buck's boat was anchored nearby.

She could see the head of someone in the water and a person standing in the boat who, she noticed, was pointing at her. The boat turned and aimed right for her hiding place.

Great, she groaned, I am one stealthy babe.

"What are you doing anyway? Are you spying on me? You seem like you're spying on me," Buck said, unzipping the top of his wetsuit to his navel.

The other guy, the boat guy, who looked like he'd spent way too much time way too deep underwater, eyed her in a slack-jawed yet thuggish way.

"No, I'm not spying on you," she said.

"What are you doing then?"

"Okay, I *am* spying on you."

"Aha!" Buck exclaimed, as if he had just pried this information from her by inserting bamboo shoots under her fingernails.

"I'm just curious, for cry-eye," she said.

Buck appeared wounded by this remark. Still, Francie plunged on. "I mean, what's all the secrecy about? Can't you just *tell* me what you're up to?"

"What makes you think we're 'up to' anything?" He sounded like the villain in a bad spy movie, only with the nasal twang of the local accent, which spoiled it somewhat.

"Because I heard you telling your dad . . ." Suddenly it occurred to her that Buck Jr. was out here goofing around with his dad freshly dead. "Sorry about your dad," Francie said.

Buck grunted.

"I don't mean to be rude, but shouldn't you be home with your family?"

"Not really my family. Buck was kind of my stepdad. My mom's ex-husband."

"Right," Francie said. "But your name is Buck, too."

"It isn't, really. It's Gerald," Buck Jr. said. "When Buck married my mom—"

"Rose?"

"Yeah, Rose. Buck thought Gerald was a sissy name so he

started calling me Little Buck. It stuck. I hated it. So then it got to be Buck Jr."

"And that's okay with you?" Francie asked.

Buck shrugged. "I guess I don't want a sissy name."

"So you and Buck Sr.," Francie said, "you weren't close?"

"Not particularly. Are you interrogating me?" Buck sounded irritated.

Francie ignored the question. Keep moving, she thought. "Listen, you told your sort-of-stepdad that you found something. Also, your girlfriend at the realty office says you've been bragging about finding treasure out here."

"She's not my girlfriend," Buck said bitterly. "How do I know I can trust you?"

"Come on, Buck," Francie said, "just tell me what you've found. Or show me. I mean, it's not *illegal* or anything, is it?"

"Fine," he said. "I'll show you, but you're going to have to be blindfolded."

Before she could protest, a bandanna was wrapped around her head. "How can I *see* anything if you blindfold me?" she cried.

"We're just blindfolding you so you don't know where we're taking you."

The boat whapped over the waves, jarring her spine. Without being able to see, there was no way to anticipate or brace herself for the worst of the waves, and she clattered about in the boat like a loose bait bucket, knocking her knee, shin, shoulder, elbow. How had the waves that had seemed so placid in the kayak become so violent in the boat?

As they bounced along, she started thinking that maybe she wasn't taking him seriously enough. He could be the killer. He had a motive—bang, ouch—his stepdad's money. He probably stood to inherit—bang, ow—something. He had opportunity.

He would have easy access to his stepdad and would know his eating habits and choices and—ouch, bang—she forgot whatever else it was she was going to think.

Oh, and one other thing: he needed money to fund this treasure hunt—if that's what it was—desperately enough to go through the realty office drawers for loose change.

The boat slowed, the motor cut out, and she felt and heard the hull scrape against sand. Then she was lifted out of the boat (apparently thuggish sidekicks are useful for this sort of thing, she thought), set down, and led along something that sounded and felt like gravel and eventually onto uneven ground and into the woods.

The whapping of the boat on the waves was replaced by the whapping of branches against her face. Thwack—ouch—she was whapped in the face by something whip-like, jabbed by something pointed, poked by something sharp. More *Mamma Mia, what have I done* thoughts as they marched through the woods. What if they're planning to do away with me and leave me back in the brush to rot?

She reflected on opportunity lost. If she got out of this alive, she would not be so impulsive anymore, she told herself. She would think things over more carefully. Look before leaping, etcetera, etcetera. She was sorry she hadn't made more of an effort to get in touch with her brother. Would he even come home for her funeral? Too bad she wouldn't get to see him.

They came to an abrupt stop—ouch again, as her shin struck against something hard.

"Ready?" the thug grunted.

24

UNDER ENCHANTMENT

"ALL RIGHT," Buck said, sliding the blindfold off Francie's face.

She blinked in the sunlight, and once her eyes adjusted, saw that they were standing next to a pile of brush in the middle of the woods.

"What am I supposed to be looking at?" Francie asked when her heart subsided enough to allow her to talk.

Buck ceremoniously lifted some dead branches off the brush pile to reveal . . .

"A log?" Francie said.

"A really, really big log." Buck patted it proudly.

"Are you kidding me?" she said. "This is a joke, right? I mean, you don't blindfold someone and submit them to beating by boat hardware to show them a dumb *log*."

Buck sighed. "Okay, you're a city girl. We can't expect you to understand this."

Francie couldn't believe she'd actually taken him seriously, when she could see what a buffoon he was. He and his mouth-breathing sidekick, Bluto.

"These are big logs and old logs, and one of these things is worth, like, eight dollars per board foot, and there's probably almost six hundred board feet in this baby. Multiply that by hundreds of these 'dumb logs,' as you call them, that are under the lake. Dozens, anyway."

"Hmmm," she said, trying and failing to do the math in her head. "Why?"

"Why are there so many logs under the lake, or why are they so valuable?"

"Both."

"Okay, back in the old days this whole area was covered with pines. Big, old white pines, this big around." He spread his arms wide. "All this area—for hundreds of miles around—nothing but big old white and red pines. They say a squirrel could run from here to Chicago on the tops of those trees and never touch the ground. They say you could have ridden a bicycle from here to there because the forest was so ancient that there was no underbrush. It musta been *amazing!*"

Francie stared at his glowing face. He was really quite articulate when he started talking about this subject, she thought, impressed that he cared so much about the forest.

"But then the loggers found them," Buck went on. He had started back down the path and Francie followed. She didn't bring up the missing blindfold. "They cut down pretty much everything. They loved these trees 'cuz they floated. They called it cork pine, in fact; it was easy to transport if there was water. They'd float big rafts of logs and send hundreds—no, *thousands*—of them downriver to sawmills to be milled into lumber. There was so much of it, and it was so cheap, that some towns had sidewalks made out of it. You know how much of that old-growth forest is left now?"

Francie shook her head.

"Less than 2 percent." Buck shoved his hands in his pockets and kicked at the ground. "It's a tapestry. It really is."

"Travesty?" Francie suggested.

"Yeah," Buck agreed. "So now the big trees are pretty hard to come by, so these logs are really valuable."

"If it floats, why did you have to pull this log off the bottom?"

"Some of them got waterlogged. They've been down there for over a hundred years."

"Okay, I get it," Francie said. "The treasure is the logs, then?" She was kind of disappointed. What *had* she expected, she wondered—gold doubloons?

They had come out onto the boat landing when Buck realized the blindfold mistake. "Craparoma!" he said. "The blindfold!"

Francie shrugged and smiled.

"Now I'm going to have to kill you," Buck said.

The sidekick, Bluto, let out a guffaw. Francie did not find it funny; her stomach seized up.

"Geez," Buck said. "I'm just kidding. You look like you just swallowed a ghost or something." He had his stepdad's way with words, Francie noticed. "Come on, get in," he said, gesturing to the boat. "I wouldn't kill you here, anyway, would I? At a public boat landing?"

Francie couldn't tell if he was joking or not, but as it was a really long walk back to her aunts' cabin—if it could even *be* walked—she climbed into the boat and hoped he was joking.

"Do you want a ride back to your grandma's place or what?" Buck shouted over the motor.

"No, thanks. I've got a kayak on the island."

"I figured you didn't get there by flying," Buck said. Bluto grunted. Another laugh, Francie assumed.

"What's that?" she asked, and pointed to a strange-looking vessel some ways distant down the lake.

"Geologists," Bluto said.

Francie turned to him. "Huh?"

"They're taking core samples of minerals."

Core samples. Where had she heard someone talking about that before? "That's weird, isn't it?" she asked. "How would they ever get the minerals out from under the lake? What kind of minerals, anyway?"

Buck and the hulk shrugged. "They're looking all over here," Buck said. "On land, too. Wherever they can get to. Supposed to be some kind of, I don't know, copper, I think."

"Just drop me there," Francie said, pointing to the island. "There's still enough daylight to paddle back."

Buck pulled up to the beach where they found her. "Where's your boat?" he asked.

"Other side."

"Oh. Now, listen," he said. "Just because we forgot to blind-fold you on the way back, doesn't mean we're not serious about keeping this secret—"

"—if you know what we mean," Bluto put in.

"I get it," she said.

"You better," Buck said, darkly. "There are others who would like a cut of this action."

Sandy, Francie thought, as she stepped out onto land. That's why he didn't like Buck.

After Buck pulled away, Francie took a look at the barge through the binoculars. It was a strange-looking piece of equipment. She supposed a mining company could afford to build a road if they wanted to. All they probably needed was a permit. What Sandy said came back to her again: seems like everybody wants something other than forest from this forest.

25
UNDER GROUND

SHE'D WASTED A LOT OF TIME on that little fiasco, she thought, as she jumped out of Buck's boat into knee-deep water, then waded onto the island. The island was just a rounded slab of granite on which enough dirt had collected over the centuries to support a small grove of red pines. It wouldn't take long to traverse it to get back to her kayak, but she still had to paddle back to Sandy's.

As she rounded the corner, she saw Potter. His boat was pulled into a small, protected cove, and he was hauling empty buckets out of his boat and setting them onto the beach.

He seemed startled to see her; he explained that he came out to the island sometimes to get clay. There was nice clay at that spot. He liked it for raku pottery. Where was her boat? he wondered. She said she had a kayak on the other side of the island. Ah, he said, he hadn't noticed it.

She climbed the rise of the island and had just started down the other side of the hill when she heard a familiar sound that stopped her in her tracks. *Ka-chink*. It was the smack and clang of a shovel hitting dirt—or in this case, clay. That was the sound she'd heard in the middle of the night. It had been that exact rhythm.

So, it had been Potter. Digging something up. Or burying something. Or whatever the heck he was doing. She tried to remain calm, but a flutter of fear ran through her and her breath came in short, painful stabs. Why? He was just digging up clay. And he had maybe been digging clay out there in the woods the previous night at 2 a.m. for some perfectly rational reason. So she should just *remain calm.*

But she keenly felt how alone she was. Goosebumps were cropping up on her arms and the back of her neck. Her scalp crawled. A sudden wind came up off the lake that made her shiver. There was a killer loose somewhere, maybe on this island. Nels's admonition to be careful came back to haunt her.

Okay. Fine. She'd just paddle home and talk to Potter later when she wasn't so vulnerable to him and his shovel.

She jogged down the hill toward her kayak. The wind in the tops of the pines made a beautiful but mournful sound. That, and the waves rushing up on the shore, made her feel lonely and a little forlorn.

Then she realized that she was going to have to paddle back in this wind and these waves. She wondered if she could manage it. But that concern paled when she arrived at the spot where she had left her kayak and found that it was no longer there. Here was the paddle, but where was the boat? Then she noticed the cheery splotch of bright yellow bobbing in the waves, quickly racing away from the island. She put the binoculars to her face. Yep. The kayak, and in it her brand-new, expensive dress, her purse, and her phone.

Crap, crap, crappity crap. She must not have dragged it far

enough up on shore, and when the wind came up, it must have blown away. Except the wind was from the other direction. Had her kayak drifted away on its own? Or had someone else pushed it off the island on purpose?

Him. Potter.

She felt as if a stone had lodged somewhere in her esophagus. She was stuck on this tiny island with a killer. *You don't know that*, she told herself.

How had he known she was here? He'd seen her at the post office. He might have followed her here and known she'd be alone on this island. He'd said he hadn't seen her boat when he went by. He could have been lying. He probably lied about everything. Her mind raced over everything he'd ever said to her. What had been a lie? What had he been mailing in those packages at the post office? Was Ginger involved in all of this in some way? Or was his relationship with her just a way to—her scalp crawled when the realization hit; her heart pounded away in its pretty silver box like a pair of fists. Was his relationship with Ginger related to T.J. somehow?

She listened to Potter shoveling, the clink and scrape of the shovel working its way into the heavy clay. Was he really digging up clay? Or was he digging a hole? A Francie-sized hole?

No, no, no, no, she thought. She had just let her imagination run rampant. Potter was just a regular guy, and right now he was her only ride off this island. She couldn't stay out here all bloody night! Her aunts were in jail, after all.

Francie picked up the kayak paddle and started to climb the hill. She would just ask him for a ride. How hard was that?

Her steps slowed as she gained the crest of the hill. She tried to talk her heart out of her throat and back in its box where it belonged.

Peeking around the trunk of a big, fat pine, she watched Potter working away at his task. His boat, pulled halfway onto the beach, bobbed up and down like an impatient horse tugging at its reins while Potter dumped shovelfuls of clay into plastic ten-gallon buckets. Maybe her Aunt Astrid had been right about the island getting smaller; after all, Potter *was* hauling buckets of it away.

Among the white pails was a smaller, squat something that looked vaguely familiar. She put the binoculars to her eyes to get a better look.

Holy crockery! Could it be? It was the very casserole dish that Astrid had described: brown pottery with images of fish on the sides.

Francie backed off the crest of the ridge in a crouch and ran down the hill to the shelter of the pines where she leaned up against one of them and let a wave of nausea wash over her. Slowly, she slid to the ground and collapsed.

The sky between the boughs was a deep, endless, and mesmerizing blue. The boughs swayed gently back and forth, back and forth. Memories of long-ago picnics she'd had with her brother on the island came back to her. He'd skip stones while she packed clamshells with the sticky sand she now realized had been clay—the coveted clay that Potter was digging up. Clay. Potter.

She felt like all the pieces of a big jigsaw puzzle were there, scattered in her brain, and all she had to do was assemble them and she would understand all this. But it was one of those crazy thousand-piece puzzles, a picture of sea and sky, with tiny little pieces, every single one of them blue.

What if Potter came looking for her? Where could she possibly hide?

Oh, to fall asleep to the drowsy sounds of the wind among the pine needles, just sleep until somebody took care of everything: solved the mystery, sprang her aunts from jail, righted all the wrongs, and came to rescue her. *I love to lie down weary / under the stalk of sleep / growing slowly out of my head, / the dark leaves meshing* were lines from a poem in that book by her bed. She didn't know what it meant, exactly, but whatever it was, she wanted it right now; she really wanted to lie down weary and mesh into the moss and old needles and dark leaves.

Maybe she could, she thought. She remembered a long time ago when she and her brother, maybe even here, had been playing hide-and-seek, and there had been no good hiding places. She had hidden by lifting up a layer of moss—as if it were the edge of a carpet—and climbing under it.

Francie rose to her knees, stripped off her sweatshirt, and laid it on the ground. She peeled back the carpet of moss and started digging. Using the blade of the paddle, she dug up earth and duff and piled the stuff onto her shirt. When her shirt was full, she carried it down to the lake and flung the dirt to the wind and waves. Then back to her grave digging. Don't think of it as a grave, she told herself. It's a hiding place. Only if I need it.

When she was finished, she crept up the hill and hid behind the big-trunked tree and peered down toward where she'd last seen Potter. He was loading buckets into his boat. Then, still holding onto his shovel, he started up the hill toward her.

Francie's breath came in short stabs. Had he seen her? As soon as he dropped his head, she turned and raced down the hill toward her hiding place. Without pausing to think about it too much, Francie crawled under the moss blanket, pulling it over her as if she were snuggling into bed. She tried to imagine herself as being invisible and hoped that, aboveground, there was not an obvious outline of a person.

The ground around her was cool and moldy smelling, a heavy

smell that brought her back to her childhood when she'd hidden this way. It had been the summer before the Accident. Her father had been very busy with something; she didn't know or remember what, so she and her brother had been left to fend for themselves, and she remembered it as a glorious summer of freedom. The smell of damp earth and moldering pine needles brought back that feeling of being a wild child of earth, a little bit animal, a little bit magical.

It made her recall something else, too, a memory as old and musty as the ground smelled. So vague it seemed like a dream, or perhaps it was. A memory of her mother. Maybe because she lay so still, she was finally still enough to feel this vibration that she felt so certain was her mother's being. Francie suddenly felt—no, she knew—her mother was still alive.

Even with a thick layer of moss and dirt over her head, Francie heard the footsteps approach, or maybe she didn't hear them so much as feel them. The ground was so soft and springy that the effect of a single footfall created a kind of wave of movement in the soft turf.

Is this what it was like to be dead, she wondered, as she lay there so still. Well, except if you were dead, you wouldn't be inhaling the dirt and duff and moldering earth. You wouldn't be feeling the rise and fall of your chest, still breathing, or the desperate thrum of your heart, still beating.

What was going on out there? Was Potter standing over her, shovel raised, about to bring its sharpened edge down? The thought made her skin crawl. Also, the thought of what might be crawling on her skin made her skin crawl.

There was a long pause, during which she tried not to breathe and, more terribly, not to sneeze. Finally, Francie felt the thump of footsteps retreating. Then silence.

After a long while, she lifted one corner of moss by her head and heard the scrape of boat aluminum on the sand, then the cough and sputter of a motor starting up, and finally the motor's buzzing hum, receding, eventually swallowed by the wind. Was he gone?

Francie waited a long, long time before climbing out of her mossy hiding place. She stood, brushed herself off, and, shielding her eyes with her hand, looked out and saw the boat, a small spot on the lake, moving away.

Now what are you going to do? she asked herself. You're still up a creek with only a paddle. You're stuck out here until who knows when. You should have taken a ride.

She'd just have to wait until somebody came to get her. Somebody would come for her eventually, wouldn't they? Sandy. He knew where she was. He'd worry when she didn't show up. Right?

Oh! But she was supposed to go to the Fredericksons'. She wondered what time it was and how much time she had until she was due there at nine o'clock. If she'd had the kayak, it might have worked out. She probably would even have had time to eat something. Her stomach was an empty breadbox.

What if she had to spend the night out here? A sleeping bag would be nice. Even a book of matches would be helpful. She felt in the pockets of her shorts and her sweatshirt: a tube of lip gloss, a small pebble she thought might be an agate. A hair tie that she pulled out and used to put her hair in a ponytail.

Maybe she could find something on the island. Kids were always coming out here to drink beer and shoot off fireworks. Who knew what she might find? She began scouring the island. A few beer cans—empty—some broken glass, plastic crap, a chunk of Styrofoam. When you started looking, it was apparent how much garbage there was. Near an old bonfire pit she found some spent fireworks and even a few unspent ones in a sealed plastic bag—a handful of firecrackers and miscellaneous stuff she couldn't identify. She didn't have any matches, but she stuffed the bag in her sweatshirt pocket anyway.

The day had been bright, but now the shadows of the trees sprawled dark and oblique across the island and left inky black splotches on the lake. Ominous clouds massed on the western horizon like an oncoming army.

Francie realized her legs were shaking. In fact, she was quivering all over. Chilly. And scared. Relax, she told herself, he's gone. I'm alone. I'm safe. She let herself sink down on the soft ground, inhaling the sharply sweet smell of sun-warmed pine needles. Out of the wind it was warm, especially here in this patch of sun. She curled up in the duff. I won't sleep, she thought. I'll just close my eyes for a moment.

But she must have fallen asleep because when she opened her eyes again, it was dark. But not so dark that she couldn't tell who was standing over her.

26

UNDER WATER

"Potter!" Francie sat up, her hand simultaneously curling around the kayak paddle.

"I'm surprised to see you," Potter said. "I looked all over for you earlier. How did you manage to disappear?"

"Magic." Francie swung the paddle as hard as she could, the blade catching him in the shins. As Potter went down, Francie leaped up and took off running.

Just where did she think she was going to go? Were they going to run around and around the island the way squirrels chased each other around tree trunks, until you couldn't tell who was chasing who? (Or was it *who* was chasing *whom*?)

She wished a tree would sweep her up into its branches. She wished the forest would swallow her. There was a favorite story from her childhood in which a fleeing maiden threw over her shoulder what she had at hand: a comb that magically grew a thick forest, a mirror that spread into a deep, cold lake.

The only thing she had in her pocket was a tube of lip gloss, which she couldn't think how to use. That and the fireworks. The fireworks could have been of use if she'd had a way to light them.

How *was* she going to get away? Run in a zigzag pattern if someone is shooting at you, she remembered learning from the fight choreographer on the show. It's harder to aim at a zigzagging target. Another bit of useless information, since Potter wasn't shooting at her. Instead, probably because of the zigzagging, he was gaining on her.

Then her foot caught in a root and she felt herself flying forward, felt her hands and arms plowing through the duff.

Potter reached her before she had a chance to even get up. "What's your problem?" he cried. "Why are you running away and whacking me and stuff? How did you get here? I saw your kayak bobbing empty in the lake, and I didn't think you were still on the island, so I was afraid—"

A series of short pops at some distance interrupted him. Firecrackers, Francie thought bitterly. Someone had a lighter. Somewhere distant.

"What was that?" Potter said.

Francie paused. It had grown darker in just the time they'd been running around the island—that dark bank of clouds must have arrived. Because of it, she couldn't see Potter's face, couldn't see his expression.

"And that?" Potter stood up stiffly, tilting his head. "What's that?"

Just barely, above the sound of the wind, Francie made out the drone of a boat motor. Coming toward the island? she wondered. No, shoot! Going away.

"A boat?" Francie said.

"No, I mean that smell," Potter said. "Smoke."

Now Francie smelled it, too. Someone having a bonfire?

Small flames appeared over the rise of the island, growing

larger and licking at the trunks of the tall pines. Sparks spurted like fireworks into the night sky.

"Fire!" Francie cried, over the crackling and snapping of the fire. "Run!"

"The boat!" Potter yelled back. "There are buckets in my boat—maybe we can put it out."

But the wind had fanned the flames into a roaring conflagration, which jumped to the surrounding brush in the moment it took Francie to turn and look. A couple of small, dead pines nearby sizzled and burst into flame. Francie leaped up and ran after Potter, holding her shirt over her face against the choking smoke.

At Potter's boat, they found the buckets, dumped the clay out of a couple of them, refilled them with water, then turned back to face a wall of flames.

She squeezed her eyes shut against the acrid smoke and flung the water at the fire. "It's no use! We've got to get out of here! Get in the boat," she shouted above the roar of wind and fire. "I'll shove off."

Potter crawled in and made his way to the motor while she pushed the boat away from the shore, then jumped in. When the motor came to life, Potter backed the boat out into the lake. Angry waves sloshed over the side as he maneuvered into the wind.

The relief of getting away was tempered by the anguish of watching the flames devour the island. Soon, though, Francie's attention was brought back to the boat, because something was wrong. The boat rocked sluggishly; it didn't seem to move properly. Then Francie noticed her feet were underwater.

"Criminy!" she yelped. "Does your boat always leak like this?"

"No!" Potter said, "I don't know what's wrong."

Francie watched as water seeped through a series of holes on the side of the boat. "Your boat has *holes* in it," she shouted.

Potter slung a string of cusswords at the wind.

"Where are your life jackets?" Francie hollered.

More cussing. "I don't know!" Potter cried. "They were here earlier."

Great, Francie thought. Just great. Well, lighten the load, she supposed, and started heaving clay over the side. Then bailing. She bailed as fast as she could, but the lake poured in while the boat rolled unpleasantly. With every swell the lake threatened to capsize them.

The boat plowed along so sluggishly, Francie wondered if they were getting anywhere. She glanced back at the island. Nearly half of it was engulfed in flames.

Overhead, the heavens announced their wrath with an enormous clap of thunder, a jolt of lightning, and rain in the form of a sudden downpour.

Oh, thank the rainy heavens, she thought; maybe it'll put out the fire. But then she realized it meant *more water*! Rain will sink us even quicker.

Francie bailed faster, but she could see she was losing the battle. Water, water everywhere: water up to her knees, more water rushing in. She was soaked through, and still the island burned.

Had they escaped being burned to death only to drown?

The hum of fear. That's what it must be, this other buzzing hum, its pitch slightly different from the sound of their own motor—more insistent, more urgent, more purposeful.

No, she realized. What she was hearing was not inside her head but a boat motor. Though when she looked up, there was just a gray wall of rain.

Then a voice shouting over the wind.

Then a tiny red light and a tiny green one, bobbing like phantom Christmas tree lights. Finally, as if parting a curtain, a boat appeared out of the storm.

27

THE PUZZLE, REVEALED

"You've got a really crappy boat, you know that?" Francie said to Potter as the screen door slammed behind them.

"It was fine this afternoon," Potter shot back. "I can't help that somebody shot holes through it."

"What?"

"Remember that popping sound we heard?" Potter said. "I think someone was shooting my boat full of holes. Soon after that there was the sound of a boat going away."

"That's true," Francie said.

"Whoever it was also took my life jackets," Potter added sullenly. "Someone with a gun."

"But why?" Francie said. "Were they trying to kill you?"

"Frenchy, you're quaking like an aspen leaf," Nels noticed, "and your lips are blue. How about you put some dry clothes on and then let's talk?"

"I think I'll just go back to my cabin—" Potter began.

"No, you will not," Francie cut him off. "Wait here. I want some answers from you."

Francie dug around in closets and drawers and found enough dry clothes for the three of them; they each went into separate rooms with their arms full.

The thought of Nels stripping off his wet clothes in the next room was distracting; Francie had to shove it out of her mind. She glanced at the clock: 9:30. She could still make it to the Fredericksons'. She paused to think wistfully of her cute new dress out on the lake somewhere, adrift in a kayak, then slipped into a pair of torn jeans, a long-sleeved T-shirt, and one of Jeannette's wool jackets. She supposed she looked bedraggled, as her aunts might say. She wished she could at least put on a little makeup or something. But all she had in her soggy sweatshirt pocket was a tube of lip gloss and a plastic bag of fireworks—not very helpful.

She swiped some gloss on her lips, crammed the tube and the plastic bag in the jacket pocket, and stepped into the living room. Potter was sulking in a dark corner, and Nels was building a fire in the fireplace. He was managing to look fantastic in an old paint-spattered flannel shirt and some beat-up chinos, both vaguely familiar—were these her dad's old clothes? That was a little too weird, and Francie looked away. Her averted gaze landed on the jigsaw puzzle on the table by the window. Her aunts had finished it, but she still couldn't tell what it was supposed to be, exactly. A lot of blue, that was for sure.

"Thanks for the rescue," she said, still not looking at Nels.

"Yeah," Potter mumbled from his corner.

"Don't mention it," Nels said.

"Were you just happening by or what?" she asked.

"I was looking for you. Sandy told me you'd taken a kayak to the island earlier in the day and hadn't returned it. He assumed you'd just paddled it back here and would return it in the morning."

"Ah," Francie said. That made sense. So much for thinking Sandy would have come to her rescue.

"But when I got here you weren't anywhere to be seen. I started to the island just as it went up in flames, and then the storm hit."

"What a bunch of bad luck," Francie said. "And I don't want to be rude, but I have an appointment with Frederica—I mean, Mrs. Frederickson—that I really ought to go to."

"Now?" Nels frowned.

"I know it's totally rude, and I can't even tell you why I have to go over there, but I do. It's really, *really* important. Potter, don't go anywhere! I'll be back in an hour." She started for the door.

"Are you serious?" Nels asked. "You're going to go make a social call right now?"

Francie turned back. Her glance fell once again on the puzzle, and she now realized that it was a picture of sky. Sky with clouds in it. Still, something about it seemed off.

"It's not a social call," she said. "I know it doesn't seem important—" Her eyes met Nels's, and she glanced away, then continued, talking as fast as she could. "This won't take long. Seriously. I mean, it could get me a job, a real job. An acting job. So, I'll just zoom over there, meet the guy, try to be charming, and then I'll come right back, and we'll figure this out."

Francie snagged a flashlight as she ran out the door, leaving two stunned faces behind.

"Back soon!" she called, as she disappeared down the dark path.

28

FREDDIE'S

THE FREDERICKSONS' DOOR was slightly ajar, so after she had knocked and gotten no response, Francie poked her head inside.

"Ms. Ricard?" she said. How should she refer to her? Mrs. Frederickson? Savery? Frederica? All these names! Francie felt like she was getting involved with a character from a Russian novel. She would have to pick a name and stick with it. Mrs. Frederickson? Or Ms. Ricard? The latter, she decided, and Frederica if that seemed too formal. But should she go in? Lake people were casual; the door was open; if it were anybody else's place, she would go in.

She stepped in.

It was very quiet. Also very dark. Well, it was a big house. They could be in any number of remote rooms.

"Hello?" she called. "Anybody home?" Her voice echoed over the terrazzo foyer.

Kitchen, she thought. I know my way to the kitchen. Francie felt her way along the dimly lit hallway and through the series of rooms she vaguely remembered stumbling into and out of with Buck the night of the party. Tonight, the rooms were devoid of guests. Here and there a lamp glowed, so at least she could see well enough to maneuver.

She was almost to the kitchen when an item resting on a side table caught her eye. Was it the shape? The size or the designs? The sharp glint of silver? She turned and stared. There, on a table under a lamp, sat a small, silver box, so like the one she imagined held her heart that her breath caught in her throat.

It was the box, the exact box she had in her memory, which she believed to have been owned by her mother. How had it come to be here, on a side table in Frederica Ricard's house?

"Pretty, isn't it?" a voice behind her said.

Francie spun around. "Oh! Mrs. Frederickson—I mean, Ms. Ricard—" Francie scrambled to remember the name she had decided to use. But all she could think about was that box. She wanted to turn and peek at it again, but the woman stood looking at her with her head tilted, waiting for Francie to finish.

What should she say? Francie wondered. "My mother had a box like that," she blurted.

"Did she?" Mrs. Frederickson said vaguely.

"I remember it from when I was little," Francie continued breathlessly, talking senselessly while her mind raced. How would Mrs. Frederickon—or Ms. Ricard—have gotten hold of something that belonged to her mother? But what if this woman *was* . . . No, that couldn't be. Her mother was dead. Well, that's what everyone *said*, but what did she have to prove that? And she'd had that *feeling* earlier in the evening, that feeling that her mother was somewhere, still alive. "But it was lost—the box, I mean—somehow," she went on. Wouldn't it be crazy if Ms. Ricard were her mother? How cool would that be? Her mother a famous stage actor? Ms. Ricard didn't have black hair with a white streak, but who could tell what color her hair really was? Wow, Francie thought, it would explain her own interest in acting—nobody else in the family was interested in theater. But wait a minute, wouldn't her own mother recognize her? Then again, maybe she didn't care. After all, she'd abandoned Francie as a baby, hadn't she?

Francie realized she'd been staring at Ms. Ricard without speaking for a long time. "Your door was open, and ... I know I'm very late. I really apologize for that. It's crazy what happened—a long story—but I just couldn't get here any sooner. I know I was supposed to be here by nine o'clock. Sorry!"

"Nine o'clock?" Ms. Ricard mumbled, vacantly.

"I thought you said to stop by tonight. I hope I'm not mistaken," Francie said.

The other woman's face seemed pale and drawn. "Did I?" she asked. "I'm sorry. So much on my mind lately. Would you care for a drink?"

"No, thanks. I'm not really legal."

"You look like you could use one," Ms. Ricard said, walking into the kitchen. "I know I could."

Ms. Ricard continued into the pantry and Francie heard ice being scooped from a bucket, dropped into a glass, then something being poured. The sound of ice rattling in a glass rattled something in Francie's memory, something about the party, but it was hard to think about that when faced with the tantalizing idea that her mother might be a famous actor, while also faced with the utterly depressing thought that the same mother had abandoned her.

"... a pleasure to see a young lady who isn't all skin and bones," Ms. Ricard was saying as she reentered the kitchen. "That's fine for television and film, but for the stage you have to be *seen*, don't you think? It's good to have some *meat* on those bones." The older woman leaned back against a counter across from Francie and stirred her drink with her finger.

The clattering of ice in her glass was so insistent that Francie couldn't help but remember the detail that had been tugging at her memory. At the party, Buck's drink had ice in it. Everyone else had been drinking bottled beer or wine out of stemware. Buck had known where all the glasses were: "There, in the pantry," he'd said to Buck Jr. And when Francie had asked for a tumbler, he had found one right away, without having to comb through the acres of cupboards in the kitchen. Obviously, he was pretty familiar with the Frederickson household.

There had been some other odd things that had happened at that party, now that Francie started to think about it, things she hadn't duly noted because she was so intent on getting near the important people, and then there'd been the distraction of the fishing incident with Buck.

"Now, darlin', what can I do for you?" Ms. Ricard said. Possibly for the second time, Francie had a feeling.

Like, for instance, Francie thought, how Ms. Ricard had known that she wasn't "a landowner—yet," as she'd mentioned to one of the party guests. How would she have known that if Buck hadn't told her?

"I don't know, Ms. Ricard," Francie said. She'd kind of lost track of the conversation.

"Call me Freddie. All my friends do." Ms. Ricard smiled her dazzling smile. "'Freddie and Frenchy.' We could be a vaudeville act." How did this woman know Francie's nickname was Frenchy? Well, it wasn't like it was a secret or anything. But still, why did she know all these things about her?

Ms. Ricard slipped a lighter out of her pocket and lit a cigarette, setting the lighter on the counter beside her. She took a drag on her cigarette, then exhaled slowly, staring at Francie through the smoke.

Francie wasn't sure what to say. "Is your friend here?" she asked.

"My friend?"

"Your friend the casting director?"

"Oh, yes," Ms. Ricard said, "the casting director." She took a few more puffs on her cigarette, squinting at Francie through her one open eye. "I'm going to give you some advice, darling. About acting: don't bother."

"Don't bother?" Francie said, rather stupidly.

"It doesn't pay."

"You must have made good money, though," Francie said. "Those Broadway shows?"

"Oh, sure! When I had work I made good money. But there are all those other times, when you're not working and wondering, Will I ever work again? Am I too old? Have I gotten too wrinkled? Saggy? Overweight? Will I never get another role? Or only the bit parts: the grandmothers—please, God!—the old housekeeper, the stern-faced schoolmistress, the old bat who cooks people into pies."

"Mrs. Lovett? That's a fantastic part! Anybody would want that part!"

"So depressing!" Ms. Ricard waved her hand dismissively. "The ticket is to have money. Money and opportunity to make more money. Ha *ha!*"

Francie found she couldn't look at the woman anymore. Her gaze dropped to the glass in her hand. It was engraved with some fancy, curlicue letters that Francie couldn't make out but reminded her of something. She'd seen them in some other context. Where?

Ms. Ricard pushed herself off the counter and strode back to the pantry. While she was gone, Francie slid her hand over the lighter. She turned it over. Yep. It was engraved, too. With the same fancy initials: F.I.R. Probably for Frederica *something* Ricard, Francie surmised. Where had she had seen those letters before? On the glass Buck had used at the party. That made sense. But somewhere else, too. Someplace unlikely.

Ms. Ricard returned, her drink refreshed, and Francie casually slipped her hands into her jacket pocket and dropped the lighter there. Maybe it was stealing, but she kind of didn't care.

Francie's insides felt watery and sloshy. As if in a dream, she realized why she'd had so much trouble understanding her aunts' jigsaw puzzle. It wasn't the sky, exactly. It was water. The sky reflected in a lake, or maybe the ocean. The clouds in the picture were just reflections of clouds. That's why it hadn't looked quite right. Simultaneously, she remembered where she'd seen that word, FIR: upside down on Buck's desk at Paradise Realty. An architect's drawing of buildings, condos or something, pools, tennis courts, parking lots, road, driveways.

"FIR Forest Development Enterprises," Francie murmured. She looked up to see the woman staring at her. Her eyes, Francie noticed, were as black as a raven's.

"Aren't you clever?" Ms. Ricard said.

"That's your company?" Francie asked.

"In a manner of speaking," Ms. Ricard answered.

The heart Francie thought had been safely tucked away seemed to be now lodged in her throat. "You're the one," she said, knowing she shouldn't say this, but saying it anyway. "You. You want to develop this side of the lake, so you had to get rid of the old folks who didn't want to sell. Get them out. It wasn't Buck who was running the show—"

Ms. Ricard guffawed. "Buck!"

Buck was just a reflection in the ocean that was Frederica Ricard, head of the FIR corporation, who was taking over the properties on this side of the lake in order, Francie finished her thought out loud, "to turn the place into a paradise of condominiums."

"Smoke and mirrors, my lovely. Smoke," Ms. Ricard said, exhaling through her nose, "and mirrors." She stubbed out the cigarette in an ashtray and said, "Let's go find that friend of mine."

She grabbed Francie's arm and pulled her along through the house. Francie knew she should struggle, but she had more questions. "You encouraged Buck to taint the well water, set the snakes free, do what it took to encourage the old folks to move along," Francie went on.

"Well, really, did you ever think Buck could have even thought of it, much less pulled it off? Such an odd man. He was really convinced that what we wanted to do was discourage them, make them *want* to sell their properties. So tedious! He was a stone around my neck. So time-consuming! Just get it over with, that's my philosophy. Move on! When I stopped getting offers for roles, when my agent stopped sending me scripts, did I just sit around and mope? No! I moved on, didn't I? I moved on to *greener* pastures, let's say."

"Was it you who set the island on fire? Shot holes in Potter's boat? Set my kayak adrift?"

Ms. Ricard chuckled, and pushed Francie down a long hallway. "I have been busy, haven't I?"

"Why, though? What do you have against me? Or Potter?" Francie struggled, but the woman's grip was like iron. Ms. Ricard was tall, Francie realized, and surprisingly strong.

"Mucking things up, darlin'," Ms. Ricard said, "In your own ways, you have been just mucking about, terrible little pigs, the both of you!" She grunted like a pig and a shiver ran down Francie's spine. Just moments ago, she had fervently been hoping she had found her mother. Now she fervently hoped she hadn't.

"Listen, sugar," Ms. Ricard went on, "let me give you the

most important advice you'll ever get: you have to know your talent! That's the most important thing: identify and use your gifts, whatever they are. Really, darling," she sighed. "It's a pity you aren't going to live long enough to find out what yours are." She opened a door to a very dark room and, without ceremony, shoved Francie inside and slammed the door.

29

OUT THE BACK DOOR

FRANCIE SPUN and reached for the handle but heard the click of a lock, then the sound of heels clattering away down the long hall in the other direction.

Stupid! She jiggled the door handle. No good. She was about to pound on the door when a voice behind her hissed, "Stop it!"

Francie spun around. Nobody.

"Be quiet and don't bang on the door," the voice whispered.

"What the—? Who are you?" Francie groped around until her fingers met a mop of dusty-feeling hair. "T.J.! What are you doing here?"

"I'm taking the pins out of the hinges," he answered matter-of-factly.

"Okay, good plan, but *why* are you in here?"

"We can't sit here jibber-jabbering! Help me with this top pin. I can't reach it. And hurry up! That lady's going to do something terrible!"

That was probably true. In all likelihood she'd come back with a shotgun. "What has Freddie got against you?"

"Who's Freddie?"

"Mrs. Frederickson."

"Hereafter referred to as the worst witch of all times!" T.J. said.

"But why did she put you in here?"

"That lady found out something—something I know about. She's going to wreck everything! I know it."

"What are you talking about?"

"If we get out of here, I'll show you. But hurry! We've got to get this other pin out. She's gonna come back!"

The pin, however, was stuck. Francie felt around on the closet floor for something—anything—to use as a tool. Ah, a shoe, a shoe with a spike heel.

"Shh!" T.J. hissed. "I hear someone!"

The sound of approaching footsteps made them freeze. Not until the footsteps continued past the door did they breathe again. Then Francie used the heel of the shoe to hammer at the pin.

"Be quiet!" T.J. said. "And hurry!"

"I can't be quiet and pound at the same time," Francie whispered.

"Whack!" T.J. said.

Francie banged away at the pin until it finally gave. Together, they jiggled the door loose from its hinges, set it aside, and stepped out of the closet. There at the end of the hall, with his mouth agape, was Nels.

"What are *you* doing here?" she said.

"Spying on you. What do you think—I'm going to let you wander around outside when there's someone trying to kill you?"

"Why didn't you come in? She was scaring the crap out of me!"

"I thought you'd be furious if I came in while you were talking. I watched through the kitchen window and saw the two of you seeming seminormal. Not weird enough to come busting in. But then she grabbed your arm, not in a friendly way, and you both disappeared. Next thing, I heard the back door slam, and I ran around behind the house and saw her stalking off into the woods. Then I came looking for you."

"The woods?" Francie said. "She's probably gone to get the splitting maul. She could be back any time. Let's get out of here!" She started through the house toward the front door—away from the woods.

"No!" T.J. said. "We have to go after her!"

"No way!" Francie exclaimed. "She's crazy. She wants to kill us!"

"You people! You don't understand. This is serious. That lady is going to the site!"

"Site?" Francie asked. "What are you talking about?"

"Ooh," T.J. groaned. "Just come with me. I'll show you. We've got to stop her! If you won't come with me, I'll go myself. I'm serious; I will!"

Francie and Nels looked at each other. Nels grabbed at T.J., but T.J. squirted out of his grasp and started for the back door.

"Okay, T.J., we'll come with you." Nels started after him. "Right, Francie?" he said, turning toward her.

"Right," Francie said. "Sure."

Nels followed T.J. out the back door.

"I'll catch up," Francie called after them. There was something she wanted to do first.

Francie jogged through several rooms, looking for the silver box, but she couldn't remember which room she'd been in when she'd seen it. After a frantic search, she realized she wasn't going to find it. And she knew she couldn't leave T.J. and Nels to face

Freddie alone. Nor did *she* want to face her alone, so she moved quickly toward the back of the house.

In the kitchen, she picked up her flashlight. As she ran past the window, she caught her reflection floating by like a ghost. Or, she wondered as she raced down the long hallway, had there been someone outside, passing by the window? She barged out the back door and smacked headfirst into—

"Sheriff Johnson?" Francie gasped.

"Potter said we might find you here." She noticed he had several deputies with him. His dog sniffed around at her feet.

Words began to rush out of her: "Oh, good! We've got to follow T.J. He knows where she's gone. We have to hurry! Nels and T.J.—"

But the sheriff was talking right back at her, not listening! "In addition to aiding and abetting—" he was saying.

"You're not listening to me!" she yelled. She thought she heard the same thing coming from him. "Stop talking!" she cried, waving her arms, which were quickly snatched up and held behind her back by one of the deputies.

"Now, why don't you tell me where your aunts are?" the sheriff said.

"Why don't you tell *me*?" She struggled against the deputy's grip, although she knew she shouldn't. "What are you doing? And what do you mean about my aunts? Aren't they in jail?"

"You know very well they aren't, and you're under arrest on suspicion of—"

Behind the sheriff, Francie thought she saw something moving among the trees. She tried to peer past the blinding flashlight beams into the dark woods. Whatever it was—if anything—disappeared among the trees.

"Look me in the eye and tell me you don't know where your aunts are."

"I can't look anybody in the eye with that flashlight beam in my face."

"'Cuff her, Deputy," the sheriff said.

"Listen to me!" Francie pleaded while struggling to stay out of the handcuffs. "There's a madwoman loose. T.J. is out there in harm's way. She's dangerous!" She tried to explain while also trying to pay attention to the sheriff. She was pretty sure she heard "resisting arrest" and possibly "impersonating an officer" come out of his mouth.

The sudden *ching-ching* of multiple sprinklers leaping to their task distracted everyone for a moment, including the dog, who tucked his tail and yelped in surprise. Francie kept her wits and bolted.

No sooner had she ducked behind the nearest shed than she felt a large hand cover her mouth and a strong arm wrap around her waist.

"Stay quiet." It was Nels.

"Shh! Both of you." That was T.J.

The sprinklers shut off as unexpectedly as they had started, and the men's voices rang, bright and metallic, through the sudden stillness.

"This way!" came a nearby shout. Francie stiffened as she heard them clattering toward the shed.

Then, improbably, a yard light switched on in the distance.

"Hey!" somebody yelled. "A motion detector light just went on in the front yard!"

The sounds of the men receded away toward the light while Francie felt herself being swept into the woods. As the voices faded, she heard the sprinklers snap on again.

"Nels," she whispered over the merry *ching-chinging* of the sprinklers, "the sheriff said my aunts busted out of jail!"

"I know."

"You knew? Why didn't you tell me?"

"You didn't give me a chance. They came to the cabin after you left. Potter told them where you were. They took their boat, and I raced over here through the woods."

"The sheriff thinks I was the one who busted them out."

"I know that, too. That's what I was going to tell you, that the sheriff was looking for you."

"Come *on!*" T.J. whined, pulling on their arms. "Hurry!"

T.J. moved like a little bear cub on a trail only he could see, while Francie and Nels stumbled along behind. There was only a thin fringe of woods separating the Fredericksons' and the bog, and they soon glimpsed an opening through the trees. They stopped and hid behind a clump of birches and surveyed the clearing.

The veiled moon cast a pale light over the old bog. Here and there, a few scraggly, lopsided tamaracks jutted up into the sky, pointy as witches' hats, while wisps of mist rose from the wet ground. Except for the occasional tapping of water that dripped from the tamarack needles and the ever-present hum of mosquitoes, it was quiet. The rain had eased up, the wind had backed down, and an ominous stillness had settled over everything.

Breaking the silence, T.J. said, "I don't think she's here. Yet."

They switched on their flashlights and crept into the bog, the beams bouncing off the uneven ground, silvering the pale grasses and flashing up into the distant darkness.

T.J. led them to a spot where the vegetation had been torn away, and Francie shone her light on it, the raw earth like a gaping, open wound. The beam caught the glint of a shovel blade, pale stones, and something slick and shiny that Francie recognized as a plastic tarp.

"What's under there?" Francie asked.

"See for yourself," T.J. said.

Nels lifted the edge of the tarp while Francie directed the

flashlight beam under it. The beam traveled along the black earth, glancing off small, stray pebbles or shiny bits of stuff, then shone on something—a root? What *was* that? She swept the light over the ground again, slower this time, and made out the shape of something that sent a creepy chill down her spine.

"Fantastic," Nels breathed. "Unbelievable!"

"What is it?" Francie asked.

"Mastodon bones," T.J. said.

Francie was struck silent as she realized she was looking at the bones of an animal that had lived . . . how many thousands of years ago?

After a few moments of silent awe, the implications of this find began to dawn on her. "Ah," she said. "Ah."

"'Ah' what?" Nels said.

"This is where the road is supposed to go," Francie explained. "Right here, over these bones. A find like this would bring construction to a standstill for who knows how long? Because who knows how many bones might be around here? They might be scattered all over the place. They'd have to do a big dig, and that would thwart Freddie's—Mrs. Frederickson's—plans. She needs the road to build her condominium paradise." What was it she had said, though? Something about smoke and mirrors? "Or whatever it is she's got planned back here," Francie finished.

"Right," T.J. said. "That's why she wants to wreck it. She wants to smash it all to pieces. She just gets rid of anything she doesn't like."

"Anything that stands in her way," Francie agreed. "Like she needed to get rid of the old folks and Buck."

"And Warren," T.J. piped up.

"Yeah," Francie said. "Why Warren?"

"Warren was going to go to town to talk to the state archaeologist who was here for a historical society thing. But the wicked witch killed him before he could get there. Warren and me thought it was only us two who knew about the site. And we meant to let the right people know, but then we realized someone else knew, somebody who was making a holy mess out of it every night. I tried to find out who it was."

"Is that what you were doing out so late at night?"

"Yeah," T.J. said. "Whoever it was worked late at night."

"I know who it was," Francie said.

"But now she's going to try to wreck everything," T.J. went on. "That's what she wants to do. We have to stop her."

"But what? What's she going to do?" Nels asked. "These bones are huge, heavy, and embedded in this muck. It's not like she's going to dig them up by herself. And even if she did, what would she do with them? Drag them away and hide them under a rug in her house?"

"She'll think of a way to wreck them. She's evil!" T.J. wailed.

"How? How can she wreck them? With a shovel? Her bare hands? How?"

"I don't know! I don't know!" T.J. cried.

"Oh, for the love of Pete," Francie said. "I know how she can do it. She's got a—" Francie was interrupted by the rumbling thrum of heavy equipment echoing through the stillness, accompanied by sounds of splintering saplings. "Bulldozer," she finished.

"Holy crap!" Nels said. "She's got her own dozer?"

"Apparently she just kept it after the house building project. Something about the lake freezing over—" The rumbling of the machine cut her off.

"We have to stop her! *Have* to!" T.J. wailed.

How, Francie wondered, were the three of them going to stop a bulldozer?

30
THE MACHINE

THE BEAMS OF THE DOZER'S LIGHTS pierced the darkness as the machine chewed its way through the woods toward them, splintering small trees in its way and crunching over logs, rocks, stumps, everything.

"Come on!" T.J. shouted. "We can intersect her."

"Intercept," Francie corrected him. Her inner English teacher would probably be the last part of her to die, she thought.

Frederica Ricard had pushed Francie's kayak off the island, started a forest fire, tried to drown her, and locked her in a closet with the promise that she wouldn't live to discover her own talents. So Francie was pretty sure the woman would not only willingly drive a bulldozer over her and her friends if they stood in front of it, she'd probably relish it.

What could they do?

Once again Francie thought of the folktale princess who, in order to make her escape, flung things over her shoulder: a mirror, a comb, mascara, a tube of lip gloss—

 173

"Hey!" she cried, feeling the lumpy plastic bag in her pocket. "I've got some kind of fireworks!" She pulled the bag out and showed it to them. "And I've got a lighter, too."

T.J. was impressed. "You've got a string of lady fingers and a coupla black snakes and—cool! A mega thunder bomb!"

"What does this mega thunder bomb thing do?"

"It's like a little bomb."

"Can it blow up a bulldozer?" Francie asked.

"Not really," T.J. answered.

"Curses!" Francie said.

Nels, in the meantime, had retrieved a shovel and set off purposefully in the direction of the rumbling sound.

"Where are you going?" Francie called after him.

"I've got an idea," he yelled over his shoulder.

"Yeah, well, I've got an idea," she yelled back.

"And your idea is firecrackers?" he called.

"Not just firecrackers. I've also got a mega thunder bomb," she shouted. "And your idea is a shovel?"

"Listen," Nels stopped and turned back toward her, "I worked one summer on a road crew, so I know at least a little bit about bulldozers. If you can think of a way to make her stop or at least slow down, that'd be helpful."

"Where'd T.J. go?" Francie asked, realizing he had disappeared.

"I hope he's well out of the way and hiding. That's what you should do, too," Nels pleaded.

The noise grew louder, and suddenly the machine appeared through the trees like some horrible monster, roaring and gnashing its teeth. Its twin yellow headlights bounced wildly off tree trunks as it jounced over the uneven ground.

Nels strode straight toward it while Francie stared after him for a moment. She intended to follow, but the sound of shouting and crashing behind her—a blur of men's voices and a yelping dog, then the high, pale, distant beams of four or five flashlights—stopped her. The sheriff and his deputies *would* have to arrive right now. She stood paralyzed for a moment. Should she try to explain to the sheriff one more time, or run after Nels to stop him before he got killed?

She could see him moving toward the oncoming bulldozer, dodging from tree to tree to stay out of sight. As the machine passed under some low-hanging branches, Francie watched as something fluttered down from the tree—something slick and shiny—and draped over the driver.

The dozer slowed as Freddie struggled to remove the tarp from her head. While she was occupied with this, Nels dashed out of the trees toward the bulldozer and rammed the shovel blade into its track. Okay, Francie thought, that was clever. But then she watched as Freddie pulled the tarp away, swiveled her head, and zeroed in on Nels, who was dashing away toward the trees. The woman shouted, then pointed something at him.

"She's got a *gun!*" Francie yelled, and before she even knew what she was going to do, Francie bolted from the trees, lighting and throwing sizzling firecrackers at the bulldozer. Whooping and screeching, she ran in a zigzag pattern, aided by the lumpy ground that made running in a straight line impossible anyway. The firecrackers went off in rapid machine-gun-fire pops. When she reached the machine, she tucked herself behind it and, using Freddie's fancy lighter, took a moment to light the mega thunder bomb, scrambled up the side of the dozer, and popped the little bomb down the smokestack.

31
THE BLAST

THE BLAST WAS IMPRESSIVE. For a moment, Francie stood in shocked stillness. When the smoke cleared, there, bright against the dark sky, was the dime-sized moon, and at her feet some bit of glimmer, as if a piece of the moon had broken off and landed there. But it was nothing so romantic as that; it was a handgun. She reached down and picked it up.

Through the misty fog she thought she saw an angel, which was really strange since she did not believe in angels. It was, of course, Freddie, who had climbed down or been blown down from her perch on the dozer and now stood a few feet from her, her wind-blown hair backlit by the headlights, her tattered clothes wafting around her like shredded wings. She was so pale as to be almost translucent and looked so fragile that Francie thought her bones would snap in a stiff breeze.

Freddie glanced at the gun in Francie's hand; Francie felt the weight of it on her palm, but she didn't raise it, didn't level it at the other woman.

Over the years it had occurred to Francie that her mother had been perhaps a very bad person who had done very bad things, and maybe that was why nobody would ever tell Francie anything about her. She had pondered the implications of that. If her mother had been a thief or a murderer, did that mean Francie was doomed to repeat her sins? And was it possible that this person in front of her now, this person who had committed despicable crimes, was, in fact, her mother?

It was remote, but it was possible. Earlier in the evening, there had been a few moments when Francie had even wished it to be true. She and Freddie stared at one another for a long moment. Some kind of recognition passed between them. Francie felt it and shuddered.

She glanced away for a moment, distracted by the yelping dog and a half-dozen flashlight beams, and noticed for the first time the ghostly winking of fireflies along the edge of the forest. That was how fireflies tried to find each other, she remembered, by sending slow, blinking signals in the dark.

When Francie looked back, Freddie was gone.

32

THE SILVER BOX

FRANCIE FELL INTO HER AUNTS' ARMS as soon as she entered the cabin. Nels and T.J. were smothered with kisses, too, and hugged to bosoms. "Thank goodness you're safe!" everybody said to everyone else in an outpouring of giddy relief.

There was a rush of excited explanations: Mastodon bones in the bog! Mrs. Frederickson the murderer! The three of them barely escaping with their lives! And questions: How did you get out of jail? Does the sheriff know you're here? And so on.

Finally, Jeannette called out over the din, "Sit down! Sit down! Have something to eat."

Soon they were sipping hot cocoa and munching sandwiches that appeared mysteriously from the kitchen. Ginger was there, hugging T.J. as if she'd never let go. Even Potter was still around, which surprised Francie. She had expected him to bolt.

Francie curled up on the couch under a blanket. Nels came out of the kitchen with his third sandwich in as many minutes and sat next to her, tugging away some of the blanket to cover his bare feet. His wet socks, along with hers, dangled in front of the fire. He slid his hand under the blanket and Francie felt his warm hand on her cold feet. He rubbed her feet into warmth, then left his hand wrapped around a foot.

"Would your girlfriend be okay with this?" Francie mumbled into her mug of cocoa.

"My girlfriend?" Nels said.

"Your date? The party?" Francie whispered.

"Oh!" Nels said, between bites of sandwich. "You never let me finish explaining. The receptionist at work wanted to go to the party. She needed a ride; I have a boat; I owed her a favor."

"Oh," Francie said, keenly aware of Nels's fingers playing with her toes. "So you don't have a girlfriend?"

"Well . . ." Nels smiled at her.

She would have liked to savor that moment, but Astrid plunked down a tray of cake and cookies on the coffee table and demanded, "Now tell us everything. Every detail. Don't leave anything out!"

Francie took a deep breath and told them about the kayak, the island, Buck, the logs under the lake, meeting up with Potter, then skipped to the fire, the sinking boat, the rescue by Nels, who got cooed at so much he started blushing. She told about rushing off to see Mrs. Frederickson, otherwise known as Frederica Ricard, or Freddie, who Francie thought might be able to help her get an acting gig. But everything turned very creepy. Francie skipped over the part about finding the silver box—she doubted now that she'd ever even seen it—to when she realized that Mrs. Frederickson ("the wicked witch," T.J. piped up) was responsible for everything.

"Buck was her—what would you call him—her sidekick? Her henchman?" Francie said. "I didn't put it together, really, until too late. Way too late. Like, I-should-be-dead late, so it's not like

I'm a genius detective; don't get that idea into your head, Auntie Astrid. I see you over there looking smug. I recognized the initials on a glass and on her lighter and I suddenly remembered seeing the same letters, FIR, in Buck's office the first day I went to town: FIR Forest Development Enterprises. I thought it was ironic that a development that would take down 99 percent of the trees would call itself FIR Forest. In retrospect, I think the FIR stood for Frederica *something* Ricard. Ingrid maybe?"

"Ingrate," Nels offered.

"Inmate!" Astrid suggested, chortling.

"Go on," Jeannette said. "Then what happened?"

Francie told about what happened next and how the sheriff showed up and tried to arrest her for breaking her aunts out of jail. "And speaking of that—" Francie began.

"We'll explain that later," Astrid said. "Go on."

"Then just as he was trying to put the handcuffs on, sprinklers and yard lights started turning on and off. It was crazy!" Francie watched as Astrid and Jeannette exchanged little smiles.

"It was *you*!" Francie said. "You did that!"

"Well," Jeannette said, "Arthur helped us."

"Arthur?" Francie asked.

Francie's grandfather appeared out of the kitchen carrying a tray of sandwiches. "It was fun!" he said.

Francie's jaw dropped.

"You were terribly clever getting us out of the slammer," Astrid said.

"*You* busted them out of jail?" Francie stared at her grandfather. Who *was* this person?

"It wasn't hard, thanks to the performance you and I put on for the sheriff earlier today."

That was a performance? Francie wondered.

"He never suspected me for an instant!" Granddad crowed.

"Well, go on dear," Astrid said to Francie. "Tell us everything."

But Francie was struck dumb. Had her grandfather just admitted to breaking his sisters out of jail?

Nels continued instead, explaining that Frederica had Buck doing her dirty work: discouraging the old folks from hanging onto their property.

"So why did she poison Buck if he was such a dupe?" Jeannette asked. "And how?"

Ginger piped up. "Here's what I think: I think Mrs. Frederickson stole Astrid's casserole dish and spatula at that potluck we had not long ago. Everyone from this side of the lake was there. I bet she thought she could poison Astrid and Jeannette with their own crockery. Which would be brilliant since she knew Astrid's reputation for," Ginger paused, "for her delicious hotdishes!"

Francie jumped in. "Ah! But then an opportunity arose to frame Astrid *and* get rid of Buck at the same time, and she couldn't resist. Remember how you couldn't find your spatula the other night when T.J. was here for dinner?"

"Mm-hmm," Astrid said. "But why? Why did she kill Buck?"

"I think Potter can answer that," Francie said.

They all turned to Potter who sat sullenly sipping his cocoa. "I'm not going to say anything without a lawyer present," he said.

"Nels is a lawyer," Francie offered.

"No, I'm not!" Nels protested. "It's just a summer job."

"Well, you work at a law firm, so close enough," Francie said, giving him a kick. She turned to Potter and growled, "Talk."

Potter sighed and said, "Fine. I knew Buck was trying to work some big real estate deal that involved getting a road through. Everybody knew about the road, but nobody quite realized how close it was to reality. Nobody at all knew what it meant. It meant the end of us! The end of this." He swept his arms in a wide circle. "Buck had bought up almost every property along the shore, except yours," he nodded to Astrid and Jeannette, who looked alarmed, "and mine. He was pestering me about it; he knew I hadn't paid the property taxes, things like that. I was broke! But I desperately wanted to keep our place. Been in my family—well, you know how it is," he pleaded.

"But your pottery?" Francie said. "I thought you did well with it."

"Gah!" Potter said. "I make crappy pottery. Nobody wants that stuff!"

Astrid let out a guffaw. "Sorry, Potter," she said, then added kindly, "some of it isn't so terrible. You made a nice casserole dish."

"I made a dozen of them, exactly alike, before I couldn't stand the sight of them anymore," he said.

That would explain why Francie had seen that same dish in different places: with the ladies and on the island with Potter.

"So, since the pottery wasn't working out, you found another source of income, didn't you?" Francie asked. "Involving ancient stone tools, maybe?"

Potter nodded. "I stumbled on a patch of overturned earth back in the bog when I was looking for clay. I found some arrowheads in there, and I started to get interested."

T.J. started up, overturning his plate. He would have had his fingernails in Potter's eye sockets if Ginger hadn't grabbed him and held him back.

"So you *were* stealing stuff! That's disgusting!" T.J. said. "It was bad enough that you were such a pig about it. Couldn't you at least have read up on dig protocol?"

Dig protocol? Nels mouthed to Francie, one eyebrow raised. She raised one back.

T.J. wasn't finished. "But no! You just rooted around in the dirt like a pig looking for bonbons!"

"Truffles?" Nels suggested.

"Yeah, that's what I mean," T.J. said.

"And that's what you were mailing when I bumped into you at the post office earlier?" Francie said. "Some artifacts?"

"Well, it was what I had *planned* to mail. If you remember, I left with the packages, the packages I had intended to send but never did."

"Second thoughts?" Nels asked.

"Yeah," Potter said. "I could have made a lot of money, but in the end, I just couldn't do it. So after that I motored out to the island, determined to get some clay (for free—I can't even afford to buy clay) and make something decent for a change. Something I can sell."

"So what about Buck?"

"When I first started digging, I was finding small stone tools, spearheads and the like. I figured they were arrowheads from a couple hundred years ago maybe. So I tried to make a deal with Buck. He said they were going to just drive a bulldozer over everything and destroy them. I said to let me get rid of the artifacts first, because if they discover anything, it'll put the road on hold until they figure out whether it's significant or not. He was all right with that idea, but then the bones turned up, and it was obvious that this was going to be a much bigger deal than we thought. He got really nervous. I think he was between a rock and a hard place. He'd invested in all these properties for something that required a road, and now the road would be stalled or have to be redesigned, which would be time-consuming. He had all his money tied into this thing—"

"And a boss who was going to be worse than grumpy about it," Francie offered.

"Buck was fretting about you, too," Potter said, pointing at Francie. "He told me later he thought he'd seen you outside late that first night you were here, as he was headed back to his boat. Everyone knew you were a detective. He was nervous about it."

Francie remembered getting up to silence the wind chimes that night. So she *had* seen a boat tied to the Olson's dock. And there *had* been someone watching her—Buck.

"But I also think he'd thought about coming clean to you," Potter went on. "I think he was feeling in over his head, but he didn't want to talk to Rydell about it. They were buddies, you know."

Maybe that's what Buck had been trying to do out in the boat the night of the party; maybe he'd been trying to explain something. "So," Francie said, "Mrs. Frederickson must have suspected he was getting cold feet, and he became more of a danger to her plan than an asset. That's why she got rid of him."

"How did she think she could get away with all this?" Jeannette asked.

"At first it was just Warren she needed to dispose of, but it snowballed: then it was Buck, Potter, and me, although she gave me credit for knowing more than I did. And also T.J. She thought if she could just get rid of all the troublemakers, she'd have clear sailing. Obviously, she didn't have much to worry about with the sheriff, since he seemed unlikely to—" She broke off when the screen door squeaked open and Sheriff Johnson walked in.

In her television series, this would be the moment the sheriff would say, "The FBI has been working on this case for months, and you almost blew it!" Or something along those lines. But Rydell didn't say anything like that. "I stopped in to say that Mrs. Frederickson has been apprehended," he said. "I also wanted to," he looked at his feet and shuffled a bit, then continued, "apologize. I'm embarrassed to say it, but you, young lady, were right—"

"No, I wasn't!" Francie interrupted him. "I told you that Buck was responsible for the deaths. And he was, in a manner of speaking, at least in some of the cases. But I was on the wrong trail."

"If I had listened to you," the sheriff went on, "and investigated, if I had confronted Buck, well, he might have confided in me and be alive today. I guess everyone knows that I've been looking forward to retirement quite a bit. Apparently some people have been taking advantage of it. Thanks, Detective Frye—"

"Oh, I'm not a detective," Francie said. "I'm really not."

"I wondered. But you know," the sheriff said, shaking his head to an offered cup of cocoa, "you could be." He gave her a little salute and went out, closing the screen door carefully behind him.

"Mystery solved!" Astrid said.

Francie watched through a fog as her aunts and her grandfather, Ginger, T.J., Potter, and Nels all clinked mugs in a toast. Mystery solved? Francie wondered. She felt an enormous mystery looming, and so many other questions were yet unanswered. The silver box. Her mother. Her father's accident. What had Freddie meant about "smoke and mirrors"?

In her TV show, all the loose ends would have been wrapped up; there'd be no mystery left unsolved. In real life, as Francie well knew, there were always unanswered questions. Perhaps there always would be.

Francie excused herself and stepped outside. The clouds had been swept away; stars shimmered in the black sky. As she made her way down to the lake, the sounds of conversation faded and silence surrounded her. She looked out at the water and the dark fringe of forest that ran around the shore, dotted with porch lights and yard lights and, of course, the ubiquitous blinking cell tower. It was no longer a wild place, but she could still sense the wilderness that stretched for miles behind her.

What must this land have been like thousands and thousands of years ago, she wondered, when the mastodons roamed here? Or even hundreds of years ago, before Europeans came and wanted so much from it: furs, timber, minerals, crops, a place to build cabins, houses, towns, roads.

A distant wail startled her; she held her breath as the moaning cry built and rose and wavered. It took a moment to realize the eerie wail came from a wolf, howling some miles distant. Then another voice and another, twining together and separating, then knitting into a chord of sound that echoed in the stillness, so mournful, as if keening for that lost world.

It made her chest ache. Everything about being here, about this place, made her heart ache with sadness yet swell with joy. Everything made it strain against its little silver box.

She turned to see Nels walking down the hill toward her, his head down. She watched him for a moment and, when he looked up at her and smiled, she felt the little box unlatch. ❧

ACKNOWLEDGMENTS

I'D LIKE TO THANK kind readers and advisors Joe Ellig, Catherine Preus, Ann Treacy, members of my writing group, and others who offered assistance, especially Kathleen Busche for her idea and advice about the crooked real estate agent.

The poems Francie reads from her bedside book are those of Wendell Berry, one of my favorite poets. Many thanks to Counterpoint for permission to reprint these excerpts.

Thanks to all the good people at the University of Minnesota Press who made this book possible, especially Erik Anderson, and to Mighty Media for the cool, clue-filled cover design.

Most important, thank *you*, dear reader, for reading!

Margi Preus is the author of several books for young readers, including *Shadow on the Mountain, West of the Moon,* and the Newbery Honor–winning and *New York Times*–best-selling *Heart of a Samurai. Enchantment Lake* is her first mystery. ❧